The Other Side Of The Ridge
New York City
September 10th and 11th, 2001

By

Larry L. Deibert

Acknowledgements

I wish to truly thank my son, Matthew Deibert, for his edits.

Thank you, Lisa Diehl for your extraordinary eye, catching many things I missed.

Diane Sismour, a fellow author in the Bethlehem Writer's Group, I thank you for opening my eyes to better ways to express myself.

My Beta reader, Ed Gibney, provided additional corrections.

Last, but not least, I thank my wife, Peggy Deibert. She has always had the final read before publishing I could never have done all this without her constant support.

Award winning author, Alaska Angelina, AKA Jennifer Bradley has been doing my covers for a long time and I thank her for her creativity.

I would like to especially thank my friend, Heather Newman, and Ellen Hart, owner of *Ellen's Stardust Diner,* for appearing in this book.

Special Thanks

There are times when one of my most difficult tasks is coming up with character names for a new book.

Last year, when our granddaughter was four, my wife and I were visiting. Not too long after we arrived, she asked us to go down in the basement where we would play a game. Nana was to be a doctor and Avery was going to be her nurse. I, of course, was to simply watch the two of them play.

Nana said, "Avery, I think this will be a fun game, but what is your nurse name, so I know what to call you?"

Without batting an eye, she replied, "I am Nurse Clarissa Fortuna."

I thought it remarkable that a four year old could come up with such an interesting name, so I filed it away, until I began writing this novel, deciding to use that name as one of my time-travelers.

The Other Side Of The Ridge
New York City
September 10th and 11th, 2001

September 10th, 2001/July 7th, 2013

1

For over four hours, time travelers Daniel Rodin and Clarissa Fortuna had been in limbo. Nearly a dozen time travelers, known as bouncers, and as many Time Travel Inspectors, soldiers who were sent back in time to watch over the inadvertent travelers, had all traveled to a warehouse in 1930 at the same time. As they waited to pass through the wormhole to 2013, Dan and Clarissa had simply disappeared when it was their turn to pass through the shimmering, green membrane that separated past from present.

When Doctor Nelson Wainwright, director of the Time Travel Facility since 2007, had seen where Dan Rodin had traveled to, after leaving 1930, he retreated to his office. He knew that his emotions would run rampant, and he didn't want the staff to see him that way.

As he watched the live video feed of his younger self and Dan in the book shop listening to Clarissa talk about her book, he reached into his desk and pulled out the autographed, dog-eared copy that he had read and re-read at least once a year, every year, since that day, September 10th, 2001. She had published the book as a novel because she could not get anyone in her critique group to believe that she had in fact time traveled. Nelson had a difficult time believing her too until she showed him several items she carried with her all these years as proof.

Nelson had dinner with Clarissa three months ago, a few weeks before she had been placed in a home. She could no longer hear, but he noticed that her eyes were sharp, and she told him she still enjoyed reading. Ever since her first book had been published, Clarissa had taken to reading books by self-published, independent authors. She had found many who were as good or better than novels by the big named authors making millions of dollars, while the indies struggled to earn a pittance.

As he focused on Dan's face, he had to smile. Twelve years ago, his friend looked the same as he did today, yet the 2001 version of Nelson never caught on to how much older Dan looked back then. Perhaps it was a good thing that he didn't, or he might have asked questions that Dan would not have wanted to answer. He was only glad that Dan was sent to 2001, or...he dared not even think what could have happened.

Nelson paid close attention to the video screen as the book shop owner introduced Clarissa. He sat back in his chair to listen to the aged writer, watching her fidget in her card table chair, trying to get comfortable. Nelson observed the expressions of the seventeen booklovers waiting for her to read and talk about her novel, *My Seventy-Five Years as a Time Traveler*. He noticed that about ten of the attendees wore quizzical expressions, and the other faces glowed with wonder in their eyes and smiles. After a smattering of applause, the aging author began to read.

On Christmas Day, 1938, which also happened to be my seventeenth birthday, I was in my parents' bedroom, trying on some of my mom's old dresses that she wanted to pass down to me. Most of the items were at least ten years old, but mom had always purchased good quality clothing and the colors were still bright after many launderings.

Trying on a bright, red dress and a pair of high heels, my reflection in the mirror convinced me that I looked older than my years, no longer a child, but not a woman either. Once dressed, I sat down at her vanity and applied some makeup and lipstick, now feeling that I looked like a movie star

After finishing, once again standing, I viewed my new look in my mom's full-length mirror. Feeling all grown up, smiling, and twirling around on the carpet, I felt like I was suddenly twirling in a dark tunnel, which really scared me. I tried to scream, but no sounds came from my mouth. My journey inside this tunnel lasted moments, or, perhaps minutes. Materializing in a ladies' room, hearing a great amount of yelling, and screaming from outside the bathroom, I stepped out seeing the inside of a stadium of some sort. Every spectator in my vision had their eyes glued to what was happening on the field. Quickly making my way toward the seats, I observed a ticket on the floor. The ticket was for today's game, September 30th, 1927, at Yankee Stadium. Babe Ruth would hit his 60th home run today. Racing to the seats in right field, I saw the scoreboard and noticed that the game was in the 8th inning, the inning that Ruth hit the famous homer.

When the Babe connected on a low fastball, the crowd was up on its feet. Their arms, flailing around me, made it impossible for me to see the ball enter the stands. However, the roar of the crowd made up for the lack of observing the record setting home run. A man suddenly noticed me and gave me a big hug. His weight caused both of us to tumble down the stairs until we were stopped by people celebrating on the stairway. He apologized profusely, thankful that I wasn't hurt. Two men had lifted me to my feet a moment before a flashbulb lit up in front of my eyes.

Finally, I was able to leave the stadium, but had no idea where I was going to go, I stepped onto the sidewalk into a sea of humanity. I had no money and didn't know where I would be able to stay for the night or even get something to eat. Seventeen years old, in a time eleven years in my past, I suddenly did not feel so grown up anymore.

Spending a night on the streets alone, knowing no one, was a real eye opener to what was occurring in the world in 1927. The Great Depression was more than two years away, but there were many people out of work. My dad was fortunate since he was a surgeon and never had to worry about not having any work. He earned a great deal of money and my family lived very well, so now dealing with the struggle of having nothing, and not knowing what would happen, I was beginning to understand how bad it was for the poor in this country, vowing that if I ever returned home, I would do everything within my power to help the poor for the remainder of my life.

The next morning before dawn, after awakening in a horse barn I had wandered into, my bed a pile of loose, fresh-smelling hay, I brushed my dress off and found my way out of the alley into the street. Meandering aimlessly, rooting through trash containers trying to find something to eat and drink, I saw a cup with a broken handle that had been tossed away, also discovering a half-eaten egg sandwich, which I devoured. Uncovering a few more scraps of food over the course of several hours helped sustain me. Passing one brownstone, I noticed a cup of coffee on the stoop. Looking around, and seeing a man step back inside the building, I grabbed it and ran down the street, turning into an alley to drink the warm liquid, feeling ashamed for stealing his coffee. Finding a newspaper, I settled down on a bench to read it. Of course, photos of Babe Ruth were on nearly every page and I was stunned seeing a photo of myself.

Continuing my preposterous journey, glancing at windows as I walked aimlessly down the Brooklyn sidewalks, I noticed a help wanted sign in the window of a small restaurant. Making certain no debris from the stable was hanging from my dress and fixing my hair with my hands, I stepped inside to inquire about the job.

The owner looked me over and seemed to be pleased, even with my slightly disheveled appearance. He asked me why I wanted this job. Responding with my recent arrival, searching the want ads, my answer was that it was simply coincidental that I was walking past the restaurant at this particular time. After he consulted with a waitress, he offered me the job and I began working that day. Inquiring about renting a room somewhere nearby, I was given an address. Rushing there immediately after work, I was able to get a place to stay. My boss had paid me for my day's work, in order for me to be able to pay for a room.

About a week after starting at the restaurant, Babe Ruth stepped inside and took a seat. Star struck, I fumbled with my words, telling him I had been at Yankee Stadium when he hit his 60th home run. From his briefcase, he pulled out a small photograph of himself, dated September 30th, 1927. He scrawled his name and personalized the picture for me by writing, 'To Clarissa, witness to my 60th home run' and he handed it to me.

I kept my job and my room for over two years, saving over one hundred dollars from my salary and my tips.

Clarissa stopped reading and said, "Because my time here is limited, I am going to skip through this rather lengthy chapter and read to you the final two paragraphs. I hope you have enjoyed this reading and I wish to thank you all for buying my book."

On December 13th, 1932, as I was walking to work, a tingling feeling raced through my body and I felt myself disappearing. A short time later, I materialized in an alley running perpendicular to a remarkably busy street. The vehicles there were not of the 1930s and neither was the clothing pedestrians were wearing. Spotting a young man with orange hair arranged in spikes frightened me and I wondered if I was still on planet earth.

Eventually I found a newspaper dated October 23rd, 1987. I was in was San Francisco, California. A new adventure was about to begin.

As Clarissa signed books and listened to the kind words of her new readers, retired Brigadier General Dan Rodin, and his friend Doctor Nelson Wainwright joined the line.

"What do you think, Nelson? Her story was certainly compelling, especially if she still has the ticket, the newspaper pictures, and the photo of Babe Ruth. I have a strong feeling that she is telling the truth and she has time-traveled." He was not about to tell Nelson that he met Clarissa in 1930 just yesterday.

"I'd sure like to believe her, Dan, but even if she does possess those items, is it possible they could be fakes? I've been a fan of time-travel for most of my life, reading a great many books about the subject, but I don't know what I would consider definitive proof that people can transcend time. I imagine that if time-travel would be a reality, the government would have the tightest lid on the means to do this. In the forward of the book, Clarissa states that in her nearly seventy-five years of time-travel she had visited nine different places in sixteen separate time periods. If she can offer tangible proof of these visits, it would certainly solidify her credibility, wouldn't it?" Nelson stared at Dan for several seconds. His friend seemed to be a million miles away and Nelson touched Dan's shoulder to get his attention.

After blinking several times, Dan felt the pressure of Nelson's hand, bringing him back to the present. "I agree wholeheartedly. Let's see if she has any free time later so we can have some time to talk with her."

As he observed the action in 2001, Nelson picked up a glass box containing a baseball signed by the man who was known as 'The Sultan of Swat'. It had cost Nelson big bucks twenty years ago, but it had greatly increased in value since then. He gently placed the $50,000 treasure on his desk and then he turned his attention back to the video screen, waiting to hear about more of her adventures.

2

After Clarissa concluded her reading and signed copies of her book, Dan and Nelson whiled away the time until they'd be able to talk to her face to face. After asking Nelson what he was doing in New York, and hearing the reply, Dan became white as a sheet.

"Dan, what's wrong? You look like you've just seen a ghost."

Recovering from Nelson Wainwright's statement that he would be in the World Trade Center tomorrow at 9 AM, fourteen minutes after the first plane would hit that tower, Dan replied, "Yeah, I'm okay, just a queasy stomach. Perhaps we could grab a cup of coffee at about 8:00 before I must leave the city. There is a great café about two blocks from the North Tower. We could have a little get together and if you leave the café about quarter to nine, you can make your meeting with time to spare."

"You know, Dan, I think I would like that. These meetings never begin on time anyway. I'd like to spend some time with you later today if you are free? We have a lot of catching up to do."

"That would be great, Nelson. Let's get together for dinner around seven. I'll make reservations somewhere and give you a call to verify." He stood up as Clarissa Fortuna approached them. Nelson quickly followed suit when he saw her.

"General Rodin, what a pleasure to see you again. Are you going to introduce me to your friend?" Clarissa asked.

"Yes, Clarissa, and remember I asked you to please call me Dan. This is Doctor Nelson Wainwright. We've been friends our whole lives."

"Doctor, it is a pleasure to meet you," she said, shaking his hand. "Let's find some comfortable chairs where we can sit and talk for a while. I have about an hour before I must move on to my third signing of the day. At my age, being an author can be most exhausting," she laughed.

They found a small nook where there were four comfortable chairs and a small table. When she sat down, Clarissa emitted a sound of pure ecstasy. "The chairs I normally have to sit in during my talks are not the most comfortable. These old bones require a lot more padding then they used to. I want to thank you both for buying my book."

Clarissa would be eighty on Christmas.

Nelson responded, "Miss Fortuna, being a fan of time travel almost all of my life, I can't wait to read about the adventures in your book. You have quite an imagination. Please call me Nelson."

She laughed. "Thank you, Nelson, but the book is not a collection of imaginary stories; I lived every moment of those accounts." She glanced toward Dan, seeing him slightly shake his head.

"But Clarissa, as much as I wished time-travel was real, we all know one cannot transcend time."

"Granted, we know of no machine that can take us back in time, but what about wormholes. Are they real? Perhaps I traveled to the past and then back home via a wormhole?" Clarissa smiled, toying with him just a little.

After a moment of thought, Nelson replied, "Hypothetically, you could possibly travel to the past via a wormhole, but as of now, that possible way of travel is merely a theory. I would like to hear what happened to you in 1987.

"I also want to hear that story, Clarissa, but would you please excuse me for a few minutes", Dan stated, rather abruptly.

3

Splashing water on his face and drying himself off, Dan stared at his features in the mirror. Although in 2001, he was only fifty-two, he did look every bit of his real age, sixty-four. Still physically fit after over twelve years of retirement, his hazel eyes did not have the shine they once had. He maintained his weight of two hundred and seven pounds on his six-feet, two-inch frame, wearing the same pants size for most of his adult life. He tossed the used paper towel in the trash bin and stepped through the door. He smiled, wondering when Clarissa was going to drop the bomb on his friend.

He returned to his seat as Clarissa and Nelson were engaging in some small talk.

"Nelson, I think you want to believe me, but I don't know if you will come to that decision until you read chapter three. What do you recall about the date October 19th, 1977?"

Deep in thought for a few moments, he finally smiled. "On that day, I was conducting a seminar at Boston University after having been invited to talk about my first book, *Time Travel In Literature.* As I recall, nearly every seat was occupied for that event and there was a great question and answer period after my talk."

She reached down to the carry bag on the floor and pulled out a copy of her book. She took a few moments to thumb to the page she wanted and then handed the book to Nelson. "Would you like to read to us, Nelson? I think you will find this section quite interesting."

He nodded and began to read her words. "When I was almost twenty-one, I traveled to Boston, appearing in a darkened hallway. Seeing light in the near distance and walking toward it, many young people were entering an auditorium. Approaching the doors, I read the poster resting on an easel just to the right of the double doors. 'Appearing tonight, Doctor Nelson Wainwright.' The poster included a picture of the young man, a Doctor of Philosophy. He was going to read from his book, *Time Travel In Literature."* Nelson paused for a moment letting those words register in his brain as Clarissa and Dan smiled.

"Doctor Wainwright shared his thoughts about some of the novels that had been written supporting the idea of time-travel and after reading select passages, he opened the floor to questions. "I raised my hand and after being acknowledged, I was handed a microphone. 'Doctor Wainwright, I too have been a student of time-travel for the past four years and my question to you is do you think that if one has the ability to time-travel, can he or she visit multiple places and time periods during a specific time."

"That is a very good question, Miss...?"

"My apologies, sir. My name is Clarissa Fortuna and I have only arrived in Boston today after spending the last two years in Austin, Texas."

Wainwright stopped reading and shouted out, "Good Lord, I do remember you now. Your name had seemed so familiar, but I could not place it. Thank you for opening my eyes, Clarissa." He stood up and leaned into her giving her a huge hug. They reminisced for a few moments and then he glanced at his watch.

"Excuse me Clarissa and Dan," Nelson said, moments after Dan had rejoined the conversation. "I have a meeting in a half hour and if I don't hurry, I'll be late. Clarissa, it was a pleasure seeing you again, and hearing your story. I plan on starting the book after dinner, but I fear that once I begin, I won't be able to stop, and I'll go to my meeting tomorrow with no sleep." He laughed. "Dan, I'll see you at dinner. Have a wonderful afternoon." He hurried out the door without another word.

"He is certainly a busy man, isn't he?" Clarissa asked Dan.

"Yes, he always has been like that. I hope his energy doesn't lead him to a heart attack. Mentally he charges full bore into whatever he is doing at the time, but he doesn't exercise enough. When we were in our teens, we were all in exceptionally good shape and I have been fortunate to keep the weight off. My fitness regimen has helped me a lot. I feel much younger than my years.

"How old were you when I met you in 1930, Dan."

"I was and still am sixty-four, having only been a traveler for eleven days, but sometimes it feels like I left 2013 a lifetime ago. Your question gives me questions. Am I in the book, and have you written about what is going to happen tomorrow?"

A look of great concern etched her face. "No, I have not included you in my book, because I only met you yesterday, yet seventy-one years have passed. I don't know what is going to happen tomorrow, and I am not going to ask. I don't think I should be privy to future events. The only thing I have done that could have changed some timelines was to invest my money in stocks I thought would grow in spectacular amounts. My investing may have taken small amounts of money from a large group of investors, but hopefully didn't change their lives too much."

"What is the latest time period you traveled to, Clarissa?"

"I traveled to 1997, and almost four years have passed since that time.

"Well, I look forward to reading all about it. Your book is quite lengthy, and I don't think I will read all night, but one never knows. The only book I ever read straight through was *The Exorcist.* I just could not put that book down."

He stood up and took her hand in his. "I hope we meet again someday, young lady." He smiled.

"I do as well. I am only seventy-nine and I have a secret desire to live to see one hundred. Perhaps I will. I hope to write a few more books, too."

"Well, I have a friend who wrote his first book at the age of fifty-two. In eight years since, he has written seven novels, so perhaps you will write many more. Good day, Clarissa and I hope every one of your book signings are successful."

"Thank you, Dan. I hope you get home someday soon."

4

Dan caught a cab and headed toward the Twin Towers. As the cab sped toward its destination, the retired general's military mind was in high gear, trying to think of a way to tell someone in a higher pay grade about what was going to happen tomorrow morning. He recalled when he had heard the news and hurried toward a TV, witnessing the attack on the South Tower as the North Tower was erupting in flames and black smoke. He could not believe what he was seeing, and thoughts of a World War began turning in his brain as the cabbie, a turban wearing Muslim, weaved, and dodged through traffic. Dan felt badly for him. The Muslim community in New York would be harassed unmercifully tomorrow and he knew the rage would still be evident in 2013. Dan's friend, Fausia Levitt had been verbally abused and her aunt, a traditional Muslim, was beaten on a street in Winchester, Virginia in the afternoon of 9/11

He recalled how he hated Vietnamese people for a long time after his war was over. Many times, he saw them dining in fancy restaurants while white, black, and Hispanic Americans couldn't even begin to think about eating there because the cost was unaffordable. He imagined that many older Americans felt that way about Japanese and Koreans living in our country. Hell, some northerners still hated some southerners a hundred and fifty years after the Civil War.

The driver stopped the car and let Dan out. He paid the fare, and gave the man a five-dollar tip, not wanting to be in his shoes tomorrow. The World Trade Center was two blocks away and he stared at the enormity of those two buildings, trying to picture the amount of human labor that went into building them.

Only a couple of days ago, he was standing on the top floor of the unfinished Empire State Building in 1930, and these towers eclipsed the height of it by over one-hundred feet. He stopped in his tracks and stared at the two structures, mentally visualizing the destruction that the world would witness tomorrow. Dan didn't know what would happen to the historical timeline, but he felt he needed to stop the planes from taking the towers down or, go to Washington and try to save the Pentagon. But, if he did that, Nelson would probably die tomorrow and then Dan might be forever trapped in the past. He ruminated for about a half an hour as he continued to stare at the towers, passersby glancing at him as though he were crazy, and then he made his decision.

5

In 2013, Nelson Wainwright watched as his friend suffered in silence, not being able to tell anyone what was going to occur tomorrow in the past. He knew Dan was trying to figure out a way to save the towers, but he also knew Dan could open up a real can of worms if he told his former superiors of the upcoming event and they would actually believe him. There would be solutions to the problem, the easiest one being to not allow the four planes to take off, saving everyone's lives. Jets could also be scrambled to take the planes down once they were in the air, but that would result in lives being taken, souls that should remain alive. He didn't know what Dan would decide, but Nelson had to be ready for anything and, for the first time since he had heard about his cancer, years ago, he was truly afraid.

He also had to deal with all the bouncers, needing to inform them that they couldn't go home without revealing the existence of the Time Travel Facility. By tomorrow afternoon, he hoped he would have a plan, but the determination of the fate of the towers would have to come first.

6

In 2001, oblivious to what was going to occur tomorrow, Nelson went to his meeting at the New York Time Travel Association. He belonged to several groups of this type, all of them within a two- hour drive from his home. He also chose groups that had many learned men and women as members, hearing their words like a sponge absorbed water. He had notebooks filled with ideas relating to the various methods of time-travel , but generally the thoughts were merely hypotheses that could not be brought to fruition.

Nelson was becoming one of the country's renowned experts on the subject matter and often fantasized about becoming the first traveler, exploring the past like a young child explored everything at his or her disposal. Six months ago, he had created a time-travel website, a place where anybody could share their thoughts about the subject. Although there were some strange ideas, Nelson read every entry, hoping to find one that could be further explored, but to date there were no viable methods of traveling back in time.

Today's speaker was Lawrence Delp, a retired CIA agent and an avid *spelunker*. Nelson read the brochure for this specific meeting and when he read that word, he had to laugh. He heard the word spelunker many years ago and he looked it up in the dictionary. A spelunker was one who explored caves, the word came from the sound a pebble makes when dropped into a deep hole with water at the bottom, He had read that the English language consisted of roughly one million words although linguists considered that that number could be off by a quarter of a million words. As he pondered the subject, Lawrence Delp stood at the podium and began to speak.

"Fourteen years ago, while exploring a cave system in northern Virginia, I was deep in the bowels of the cavern, seeing a green glow about fifty feet away. Drawn to it, I slowly traversed the rough terrain to an arm's distance away from it. Seeing the pulsations, I held my arm straight out in front of me, watching as my fingers and then my hand and my arm up to my elbow disappeared. I pulled my arm back out and checked out my skin to see if there had been any change to it after performing this maneuver. My arm looked fine, and as I went over it with my other hand, it felt the same as it always had. *My God, Lawrence, you've found a wormhole,* I shouted out loud, thrilled with my discovery.

"Next, I braced my hands against the walls beside the small wormhole and stuck my face through the green, watery membrane. Opening my eyes, seeing a town in the distance, I stepped through the wormhole.

"After taking a couple of steps, I turned around and saw the base of a mountain. I piled some rocks at the exact spot I had walked through it, hoping the wormhole would reappear when I returned from my exploration.

"I walked the short distance to the town and smelled coffee brewing. Standing in front of the New Columbus Restaurant, I saw a newspaper lying on a bench. I picked it up and saw the date, May 28th, 1933, and New Columbus was in Maine. My problem was that I had no money that would pass in 1933 so buying anything was out of the question. My backpack was OD green so I thought that would pass and my clothing also would not appear out of place. I did have a couple of plastic water bottles in my pack, along with a new novel, published in 1986. I carried a spiral notebook and ball point pens. Basically, everything I carried would be an anachronism in 1933.

"Many of the buildings in the area were in bad states of repair, so I figured the town was going through a rough time, since it was in the middle of The Great Depression. Stepping inside, I asked if there were some chores I could do to earn the cost of a meal. As luck would have it, the dishwasher had called in sick and there were a ton of plates, cups, forks, spoons, and knives that needed washing. Two hours later, I had them all finished and was rewarded with a plate of eggs, home fries, toast, and bacon, along with unlimited coffee.

"I was asked if I could stay for the day and do the dishes for the lunch and supper meals, and if possible, could I stay on tomorrow as well. I was offered a small room behind the dining room and it was quite comfortable.

"After my day's work was done, I was fed again. The owner of the restaurant gave me a dollar and told me to go to *Shorty's Bar* and have a couple of beers to relax. While at the bar, I conversed with some of the town's men. Many of them worked at a granite quarry twenty miles away, one of the few places that was fully employed. The pay was good, even though the hours were long, and the work was hard.

"When I finished my work the following day, I had a bite to eat and thought it was time to go home. Dishwashing was something I could do without. I found the wormhole, but it was closed, and I didn't know if it would open automatically in my presence or not. When it didn't, I rubbed my hands on the stone of the mountain until the wormhole opened, allowing me to step through it into the cavern. After traversing my way back to the cave's entrance, I found myself back in 1987.

"My former coworkers laughed when I told them this story and I had no way to prove it. I've been trying to get someone to believe me for fourteen years, but I still have had no takers. If you think I am telling the truth, meet with me at the conclusion of this meeting and I will talk with you."

7

As Dan stared at the Twin Towers, many things were flashing through his mind. At this moment, he was mentally back in Vietnam, reliving the day that he, his twin brother, Harry, and his friend, Will Jennings, could have easily been killed.

The platoon had been patrolling for several days, coming into contact seven times with small bands of Viet Cong. Due to this heavy activity; he radioed headquarters reporting that they might be nearing a VC stronghold.

After he got off the horn with the old man, he walked over to sit with Harry and Will. They looked up as he approached. Despite being a friend and a brother, he was also their commanding officer, and they gave him due respect for his rank.

"Hey, LT, what's going on?" Harry smiled at his brother.

Dan sat down on the hard-packed ground and lit a cigarette. "I just called Captain Lowell and told him about what's been going down the past few days and that we suspected we might be nearing a VC stronghold. The old man told me to hang tight right here and he would send in another platoon before we continued on. I have a bad feeling we're going to get in some really nasty shit before this is all over." He looked at them, waiting for their comments, comments he valued highly.

Will continued whittling a stick with the brand-new pocketknife his folks sent to him in the mail. "You know, LT, you may be right. The hairs on the back of my neck have been standing up almost all morning. I think we're close, and Charlie's going to leave us alone until they get us in a kill zone. They probably figured you'd call the company for more men. It's going to be a turkey shoot for them." He looked up into his friend's eyes. "Dan, I don't want to die in this godforsaken place."

He nodded and then looked at his brother.

Harry pursed his lips. "I think Will is right. A lot of us will be going home in bags in the next day or so, and I don't want that to happen to anyone, especially the three of us. We have too much to do with our lives to have them end here in Vietnam. Plus, we are getting much too short for this shit." A wry smile crossed his face. The three of them had come to 'Nam together and had less than thirty days to go before heading home. They knew about the rule that two brothers could not serve in combat at the same time unless they volunteered. They volunteered to go together, and Will was not going to let them go without him.

Dan closed his eyes for a moment and thought about home, their parents, and friends. He watched Will whittle, admiring the knife in his hands. "When did you get that knife? Can I see it?"

After retracting the blade, he flipped it to him. Dan opened it, tested the edge of the blade with his hand and whistled. "Sucker's really sharp." After closing it, he threw it back.

"Yeah, I just got it a couple of days ago from my dad, and he put a hell of an edge on it before he mailed it."

Harry pulled back the charging handle of his weapon and checked the chamber. "Guess we're going to really get into some heavy shit soon."

In the distance they all heard artillery rounds exploding, alerting them to the fact that more Americans and Vietnamese were in heavy combat. Moments later they also heard the staccato of automatic weapons fire; the AK-47 emitted a deeper sound, while the M-16 was thinner. To Dan, it sounded like there were more M-16s being fired than AKs.

Dan rubbed sweat from his eyes with his dirty hands and nodded "'Fraid so, brother. Listen to the firefight in the distance. Headquarters sees this clusterfuck as a chance to catch the VC where they live, but I'm sure that with only eighty-four men we are going to be outgunned at least three to one, plus the gooks are going to be dug in pretty good. Cobras will get some, but there's going to be plenty of VC for us to kill, or," he paused, "to kill us."

Moments later he heard multiple rotors about five minutes out from the platoon's position. He stood up, looked at his friends and said, "Time to go earn our pay, guys." They followed him to the LZ to hook up with the rest of the men.

After the slicks landed, three Cobra gunships took off toward the suspected VC stronghold. The men now walking toward the jungle heard miniguns, rockets, and AK-47 fire in the distance.

Fifteen minutes later, after the Cobras softened up the area, the men spread out on line. Dan stumbled across a couple of dead enemy soldiers, uniformed NVA, amidst trees torn and ripped apart by gunfire and rockets.

***

VC soldiers, well concealed inside camouflaged bunkers and tied to the upper branches of trees, watched the Americans approach. When the firefight began, the platoon had seen numerous muzzle flashes, but no visible targets. Several men died in the first burst before the rest of the platoon found cover. The gunships returned and laid down a heavy volume of fire from above the treetops, killing some more of them, but it wasn't enough. As Dan fired his M-16, he saw a half dozen gooks pop up from spider holes on his left flank. They charged toward Will and Harry. Dan stood up and killed all six of the enemy before they could harm his friend and brother. He moved closer to the bunkers, tossing grenades and spraying the Communists with his M-16. More men charged the enemy positions and killed many of the slant eyed bastards, but three more Americans died. Dan then took out the machine gun emplacement with rifle fire and a well-placed grenade.

About a half hour later, the remaining enemy soldiers disappeared into tunnels, spider holes, and the thick jungle. The fight was over. American losses were twenty-four dead, seventeen wounded, and one missing.

The platoon swept the area and counted one hundred and seventeen dead gooks. Eighty- three enemy weapons were found and stacked for destruction.

***

Dan sat on a log and lit a cigarette. Harry and Will came over to join him.

"Damn, LT. You were like a maniac out there, but if you hadn't charged those bunkers, and got us to follow you, a lot more of us would probably be in body bags now." Will took out his pocketknife, etched LTDAN in the handle with another knife, and gave it to his friend. "Hey buddy, this is yours now. You earned it for saving my bacon today."

Dan grinned and accepted the gift. "This will never leave my person, not ever!"

However, when he was searching for artifacts near Chambersburg in 2013, he was whisked back to 1863 and he dropped it, hoping Will would come looking for him and find it.

8

After the meeting, Nelson, along with Saundra Mason, Melanie Cullen, and Stephanie Williams, was ushered into a small room where there were pastries and coffee. The three strangers grabbed some food and drink and sat down waiting for the arrival of Lawrence Delp. He was still taking questions from several people who had approached him, and the foursome hoped it wouldn't be too long before he came in to talk with them.

A few moments later, Lawrence entered the room and took a seat. "HI folks, you all know about me, now how about telling me about you."

"Sure, I'll get my feet wet. I'm Saundra Mason from Kokomo, Indiana. I'm 32, single, and I graduated from Marcel Lafayette College with a degree in graphic design. For the past nine years I have worked for Lorenz Graphics in Philadelphia, Pa. I was very intrigued when I received an invitation to this seminar, and I look forward to learning more about your adventures, Mr. Delp."

"Thanks, Saundra. Please call me Lawrence. Who's next?"

A tiny woman jumped from her seat and introduced herself. "I am Melanie Cullen, but you can call me Mel. I'm 23, been married twice and divorced twice and I have no kids. I just graduated in June from Columbus University in Maryland with a degree in library science." She sat back down, and Lawrence had to momentarily turn away from her. Her skirt had risen to where it was the length of short shorts and he could see her pink panties. A moment later, she crossed her legs and he focused on her dainty feet encased in pink and blue flip flops. Her long red hair was tied back in a ponytail and she sported large, purple-tinted glasses. She had a radiant smile with perfect teeth, and for a moment Lawrence wished he were fifty years younger.

Stephanie Williams stood up. "Hi everyone, I'm Steph Williams. I'm fifty-seven and I am a retired letter carrier. I hold a degree in teaching, but after doing that for one year, I found that being in a classroom with thirty snot nosed kids for seven hours a day was not for me. I originally hale from Hadleysville, North Carolina, but I transferred to New York City when I was in my mid-thirties. I thank Lawrence for sending me a special invitation to attend his talk today."

Last, but not least, Nelson Wainwright stood up and after introducing himself, he told them what he did for a living and how impressed he had been to receive an invitation as well. He sat back down and gave Lawrence the floor.

"I have selected the four of you to come here, knowing you all had open minds to time-travel. Folks, I really did travel back to 1933 and we have been working on building a facility inside the mountain with the worm hole. To date, I have been the only one to travel back in time, and I have done it sixty-three times since 1987, traveling to a different place and time each trip. I am here to offer you four jobs at the facility and to help us work on the key to open the portal for anyone inside the facility to travel back. You can refuse, but you cannot divulge anything I have spoken about today. Each of you will receive a ticket on the next train to a location near the facility. The windows will be covered so you cannot see exactly where we are going and when the train stops, you will be blindfolded until you are inside the facility. I'm now asking you to leave and not speak about this to each other, nor anyone outside this room. I hope to see you four on the train tomorrow and then we will discuss this more. Have a great day. If you choose not to participate, have a great life."

9

Dan came out from his reverie when he heard a horrible crash and smelled smoke. He turned and saw that a cab had crashed into a postal truck. Unbeknownst to the mail carrier, the truck had a gas leak and, when the cab hit it, the gas on the street was ignited by a spark and both vehicles were burning.

A man rushed to the cab and yanked open the back door, grabbing the stunned passengers, a middle-aged woman and her companion, a boy of about twelve, pulling them from the impending inferno. After they were safe, he raced to the other side of the 2000 Caravan, pulling the unconscious driver into the street, dragging him a safe distance from the vehicle as three police officers arrived at the scene.

The man saw the postal worker hop out of the truck, carrying a fire extinguisher, probably thinking that he could put out the fire and save the mail. Dan ran over and grabbed him, dragging him away from the flames. He screamed, "Man, don't worry about the mail, save your ass and get away from this fire." He then heard the fire engine coming down the street and prayed it would be on time to control the fire and put it out.

When the dangerous situation was diffused, Dan took a closer look at the person who performed the rescue. It was him! How could his 2001 self and his 2013 self-share the same time and space? He was mystified by this anomaly.

10

The staff in the TTF were also stunned, wondering how a person could share the same space with his younger self. They all knew that they had to stop the two Dans from getting any closer, thinking that one of them could possibly die. As they watched, Ken and Arlen went into action shouting commands to open the portal so they could go back and keep the Dans apart. The 2013 Dan began to walk across the street, getting closer to the 2001 Dan with each step.

In seconds there was enough power to send the TTIs

A tech shouted out, "I don't know where you are going to land, and I wish you guys luck." He was afraid that there could be a cataclysmic effect if the two Dans got too close; however, what was too close?

11

2013 Dan continued walking toward his younger self, not even thinking of any repercussions that could occur. After taking two more steps, Ken appeared beside him and grabbed his arm, turning the retired general around. Before they started walking back to the sidewalk, Ken saw Arlen walk up to younger Dan who was still in shock after saving those peoples' lives.

"General! What a surprise seeing you here," Arlen said, getting young Dan's attention.

Dan looked at him and replied, "Do I know you?"

"Yes, sir, I served with you three years ago."

Dan shook hands with him, still not remembering him, but he hoped that his memory would kick in soon.

"What brings you to New York, Sir?"

"To be perfectly honest, Arlen, I don't know. I don't remember coming here and I was kind of in a daze until this accident happened. I think I came by bus, though."

"That would be easy to figure out. Check your wallet or pockets for a return ticket."

"Good idea." He pulled several things from his pockets, but none of the items was a return ticket. He took his wallet from his back pocket and opened it. There, in with his cash and credit cards, was a return ticket."

"Okay, now we know you came by bus, but why you are here is the question we have to try to answer." Arlen looked across the street and saw Ken and Dan looking toward them. He motioned for them to go somewhere else, not wanting Dan to see his older self. His memory was filled with holes about today and he didn't want to make it worse with an old Dan sighting.

12

Ducking into a nearby McDonalds, Ken and Dan found an empty table and sat down. It didn't matter what time of day it was, restaurants of every type seemed to always be busy in the city.

"General, can I get you something to eat or drink?"

Lost in thought, it took him several moments to respond. "Thanks, but no. I'm good. Go get something for yourself, though."

"Thanks, I will."

After Ken left the table, Dan tried to recall what he had done all morning before arriving at this location and he drew a complete blank. He considered calling his brother, Harry, but he couldn't remember a number he had called hundreds of times in the past.

Ken returned to the table holding a tray with two burgers, two fries and two Cokes. "Just in case you changed your mind, General," he said.

"When was the last time you saw Harry, Ken?"

"Yesterday," he replied. Why?"

"I can't remember his cell number. I was going to call him to see how he was getting along. I haven't seen my brother in a couple of months." He was animating with his hands and Ken gently grabbed them and placed them back on the table.

"Dan, what do you remember about Gettysburg?"

"That's a strange question. I haven't been to the battlefield in years, but I guess it hasn't changed. Why did you ask me that?"

13

The total silence in the TTF spoke volumes to what they were all hearing.

Nelson was extremely concerned as he listened to the conversations. Both Dans were having memory issues and they seemed to be getting worse with each passing moment. Harry stood beside him and he was afraid for his brother.

Harry put a hand on Nelson's shoulder and said, "Nelson, Dan was nowhere near New York City in 2001. He and I were at a Vietnam veteran reunion in Connecticut where we watched the 9/11 drama on TV. I don't understand how he is in the city now and sharing space with his older self. This is way above my pay grade. What are we going to do, Nelson? I don't want to lose my brother. Would it help if I went back?"

Nelson shot him a stern look. "Absolutely not. I don't think it would do any good to put you in a situation with your younger self being in Connecticut. Trust me, Harry," he smiled looking at his friend, "This is way above my pay grade too. We are in uncharted waters here and I don't know what to do."

Although Harry was terribly upset, Nelson turned his attention back to the video screen watching his brother's younger self talking with Arlen.

"You know, Arlen, this has never happened to me before. My memory has always been superb, and now..." His voice trailed off.

Arlen asked him if he had a smartphone.

"What in the hell is a smartphone, Arlen?" Dan inquired.

Forgetting he was in 2001 and not 2013, Arlen thought quickly. "Sorry, Sir, but a new phone has just come on the market in the past couple of weeks and they call it a smartphone because of all the applications it offers to the user. I'd show you mine, but I forgot it in my car. I was charging it. Is your phone capable of getting the Internet?"

He pulled it from his pocket. "I don't think so. Would you like to check it and see if I have access?"

Arlen took the phone and looked for an app. He couldn't find one, but he did find Dan's address book. Hoping to jar his memory, he opened it and handed the phone back to the general. "Do you recognize all of the names? Maybe you were supposed to meet someone here in the city."

Dan scrolled through the list, seeing names of former soldiers he served with and one name really jarred him. "This guy was my sergeant major in Vietnam. I remember I was supposed to be in Connecticut around this time for a reunion, but I don't quite remember the dates. Do you think I should call him, Arlen?"

"I do, Dan. You could tell him you're calling because you aren't sure of the dates of the reunion and tell him that since sergeants major never forget, you figured you'd ask him."

Dan smiled. "Yeah, that's a good idea. Top's memory was always sharp as a tack." He dialed the number.

14

Retired CSM Will Robinson was enjoying himself at the reunion. He had already spoken to five or six of his men from Vietnam, finding out that they were all in surprisingly good shape physically and mentally as well. Robbie, as he was now called, was telling stories about his army career. He was 77 years old, but he was still the same weight as when he joined the army in 1952, one-hundred and seventy-two pounds carried on a five-foot eleven- inch frame. His muscle tone was that of a man fifteen years younger. He still had twenty-twenty vision and all his teeth. After Vietnam, no longer working in the field but driving a desk, he was promoted to Command Sergeant Major for the 186th Light Infantry Brigade stationed in Germany.

As he sat down in a lawn chair outside of his mini Winnie, gnawing on a chicken leg and drinking a beer, two men approached him, smiling when they saw the flag hanging from the awning of his vehicle. It was the rank symbol of a CSM on a blue field, the color of Infantry.

"Command Sergeant Major Robbie Robinson, Staff Sergeant Harry Rodin and Specialist Fourth Class Will Jennings reporting for food and beer."

"Hello, men. Food's on the grill and in the plastic Tupperware and beer is in the cooler. Help yourself. Where's the LT, excuse me, the general?"

After fixing a burger and grabbing a beer, Harry sat down beside his old top sergeant. "Beats me, Top. I haven't seen him since late afternoon yesterday and he doesn't answer his phone. You know how my brother can go off sometimes for long periods of time and not let anyone know."

"Yeah, don't I know it. One day when we were back at the base camp in 'Nam, he took off for parts unknown. Captain Smothers looked for him almost all day and I just kept telling him that Dan was probably on a mission. When I finally saw him near dusk, he was totally shitfaced and smiling like he just heard the world's best joke. Damn officers, Harry. He went to the 'ville, alone, and I assume he got laid, but he never would tell me what he was doing there. When he reported to Smothers, he lied his ass off. The yarns that he could tell were enough to make this old sergeant major blush like a teenager pulling some stunt and getting caught."

Will Jennings sat down, and Robbie looked at his plate. "You going to eat all that, young specialist, or is old Robbie going to have to dress you down like back in the day?"

"Don't worry, Top, I got this." He started eating and just kept stuffing his mouth after each bite. Two chicken legs, a burger, and a hot dog, plus three beers later, he belched loudly and shot Harry and Robbie shit-eating grins. "Good stuff, Robbie. Thanks."

When Robbie's phone rang, he picked it up, saying, "Hello, this is Robbie."

"Robbie, hi. This is Dan Rodin."

Harry and Will saw a look of surprise cross Robbie's face and then heard him say, "Dan, I'm sitting here with your brother and Will. Where the hell are you?

"I'm in New York City and I have no idea how I got here and where I had been before getting here. I guess since my brother and Will are with you, I'm missing out on something?"

"Dan, it's Harry," his brother said after taking the phone from Robbie. "We're at the reunion and you left without letting any of us know where you were going. Are you coming back soon?" He didn't want to ask why he went to New York City.

"I guess I will be coming back, but I don't know where you guys are. My mind is like Swiss cheese right now."

After telling Dan where they were at, Harry handed the phone back to Robbie. "I think my brother is having some serious issues and when he returns, I'm going to have him see a doc to find out what is happening with his memory."

"Good idea," Robbie stated. "Our former medic came back, went to medical school and has been a doctor for over forty years. He's here at the reunion so maybe he'll take a look at Dan when he gets back."

15

A half hour later, after hopping on a train, Dan began to feel better. He remembered going to the reunion with Harry and Will and getting on a train to New York City. He still didn't recall why he did this, but as more and more memory cells reawakened, he recalled assisting people from harm's way after the crash and his hands flew to his mouth, stifling what was going to be a scream as he remembered seeing an older version of himself walking across the street toward him, before the man named Arlen turned him around and introduced himself.

Dan's lifelong friend, Nelson Wainwright, spoke often of the possibility of traveling through time. *Was the older version of myself a time-traveler? After this reunion ends on Sunday, I'm going to go see Nelson and have a long talk with him.* Dan began to feel better and he was certain that most of his memories had returned. He turned and looked out the window at the fast-moving scenery.

16

Back in the city, Dan Rodin the time-traveler found his memory returning as well.

When he realized when and where he was and who was sitting across from him, he finally cracked a smile. "Oh, Ken, I am so sorry I forgot who you were. What the hell happened to me?"

"What do you remember about today so far, Dan?"

"I recall being in a warehouse here in the city in 1930 talking to a bunch of travelers and TTIs, hoping that since we were all gathered together, we'd be sent back to 2013 en masse. After the wormhole opened, everybody started passing through to the future one at a time until Clarissa Fortuna and I were the only two remaining. I remember that she had taken a step toward the portal, but a moment before stepping through, she disappeared. Not wanting to miss my opportunity to come home, I lunged for the green membrane and was certain I had touched it when I disappeared as well.

"Finding myself standing on a busy street, staring at the towers of the World Trade Center, I knew the date to be sometime before 9/11. A newspaper in a trash can was dated September 10th, 2001. Tomorrow would be hell on earth.

"I was laughed at, still wearing my 1930s style clothing, Figuring I should probably buy some contemporary clothing, I looked in my wallet, seeing fifty-three dollars, all in old money that might not be accepted in stores. I went to a bank to get them exchanged, but the bank manager sent me to a different place where I was given over three hundred dollars for the old bills."

At that moment, Arlen Behr walked in, causing Rodin to smile again. He had first met Ken Younes and Arlen on June 27th, 1863 at Robert E. Lee's encampment near Chambersburg, Pennsylvania, which had been only eleven days ago in real time. Dan stood up and shook Arlen's hand.

"I heard you telling Ken a story and I'd like to hear the rest of it before we begin talking about today, if that's okay with you, General." He sat down.

After sitting down again, Dan said, "That's fine. You didn't miss much, but I'll repeat what I told Ken.

"...so, I went to a clothing store and bought slacks, a shirt and a pair of modern-day loafers and as I walked down the street, I noticed a poster board outside a bookstore announcing a signing that day at one PM. There was time to grab a bite to eat before the event, so I walked into a nearby restaurant. Several minutes later, after I saw him enter the restaurant, Nelson Wainwright joined me at my table. He was planning on going to the book signing as well because the author was Clarissa Fortuna.

"We chatted for a bit and then I asked Nelson why he was in the city. When he told me he was going to a meeting at the North Tower tomorrow, I nearly crapped my pants. He's going to have breakfast with me in the morning, but I don't know how I can talk him out of going to the meeting without telling him I had time-traveled here.

"Arlen, I had seen you across the street with my younger self. How did this happen? I thought that in time-travel one could not share the same space with himself?"

"Apparently fiction writers only thought that sharing the same space with yourself would cause cataclysmic events in the historical timeline. I guess we'll find out when we return to 2013."

"Okay, so why has my memory suddenly returned?"

"When I was with your younger self, I tried to find out where he had come from and after calling your old sergeant major, he realized he had left his reunion in Connecticut, so he decided to get a train and head back. I can only assume that as he walked further away from this location, the separation broke the bond and you are remembering more each minute. I can only guess that the same thing is happening to younger Dan."

"I remember that reunion very well. Sadly, Robbie died a couple of years ago. He and his wife were driving on an icy road when the car began to slide toward a flatbed trailer carrying a load of steel beams. Knowing he wouldn't be able to stop the car in time, he pulled his wife down, saving her from certain death. He died a hero, just like he had lived. He was a great guy. I remember another time when I was cleaning out a desk drawer and I found a slip of paper with a phone number on it, but I didn't recall whose number it was. I called and introduced myself, saying 'I don't know who I am calling but my name is Dan Rodin.' His booming voice filled my ears saying, 'LT you better be at attention when you're talking to your sergeant major.'"

"I think I would have enjoyed working for him, Dan," Ken said. "So, how are we going to save Nelson's life tomorrow?"

17

In the Time Travel facility in 2013, Nelson Wainwright devoted his full attention to the conversation between his two TTIs, and Dan Rodin. As of now, he was still alive, but would circumstances change tomorrow? Would he reconsider coming here to the TTF, where he would work for the remainder of his professional life, or would he instead, walk to the North Tower and be inside the building when it would be struck by a plane at 8:46 AM? Prior to seeing what had occurred when Dan and his younger self were in close proximity, he had considered going back to 2001 to save himself from certain death. The office he would have been in was totally destroyed when the plane hit, and even if it would not have been, he didn't know if he would have been able to get out of the building before it collapsed.

Still deep in thought, watching the video feed from 2001, he was approached by a technician. "Sir, Beverly Fair is in her room waiting for you to interview her."

"Thanks, please inform her that I will be there shortly."

He returned to his quarters where he took a few minutes to refresh himself, washing his face and hands. He felt like he was sweat covered everywhere, even in the climate-controlled facility, but at least after washing his face, he felt a little more reinvigorated. He strolled a couple of doors down the hall, knocked and heard, "Come in."

Thirty-seven-year-old Beverly Fair sat in a comfortable high back chair; her long legs crossed. She was wearing a powder blue sweat suit and her lengthy blonde hair was tied back in a ponytail. Her lips were the color of pink roses and her blue eyes sparkled. Her smile was radiant with nearly perfect, snow white teeth. "Please come in, and sit, Dr. Wainwright. I am anxious to tell you my story.

"I was born in 1976 during the height of the disco craze. I think my folks had come home from a party and had some fun, not expecting me nine months later.

I led a relatively normal life as a kid, being involved in many things our community and school offered, immersing myself in 4-H, Home Ec, Debate Club, and Library Club. I was a bando, playing triple drums for four years in high school, the only percussionist in our school to ever become senior prom queen. After graduating with straight A's, I went to a local business college, getting a degree in Business Administration, which didn't really mean shit when I went job hunting after graduation.

Not knowing what to do with my life, I joined the army, enjoying military life, working as an Administrative Support Specialist. My ultimate goal was to procure a civilian job in this field after my four-year commitment. All my life I had been a number freak and, in all my clubs, keeping the records of members, their abilities, and their finances. It was fun seeing a sheet of paper with nice straight lines filled with numbers and facts.

When my four years were up, the army offered a nice bonus to sign up for another three years, so I took it. Not only did I have a job I liked, good friends, and decent food, I was able to maintain my weight by working out. I formed a four-piece rock band. We played a lot of sixties music which was really my first music love.

I had been at the same duty station for five years, when one evening, as I was walking back to my barracks in a thunderstorm, my entire body tingled and I raced toward a bus stop hoping to get a little protection from the heavy rain and hail, as lightning strikes were hitting nearby. I can't tell you how scared shitless I was at that time. I was twenty-five and at that moment I didn't think I'd see twenty-six.

I plastered myself to the wall in that little bus stop and cringed, crying like a baby, and screaming at the top of my lungs at the same time. A bright flash went off behind me and then there was absolute silence. I opened my eyes and found myself standing in a wooded area just on the outskirts of a small town, more of a village, perhaps.

There were small houses, a store, a church, and in the center of the town stood gallows with a knotted rope hanging over the middle of the platform. A set of wooden stairs led upward to the platform. Staring at it, wondering where I was, a group of people approached it. Several men and a hooded woman climbed the steps and when they arrived on the platform, they placed the noose around the neck of the woman. I had to cover my mouth so as not to scream. One of the men read words printed on what appeared to be parchment paper and then two other men tightened the noose. One of the men strolled to a lever and a section of the platform under the woman's feet opened. She fell through and I heard the bones in her neck break. She squirmed and wiggled for a couple of seconds and then the body was still.

The crowd cheered, except for a young man with three children, two girls and a boy, none probably not older than six or seven. Those four cried. The men hauled the body back up onto the platform, closed the trap door and removed the noose from the dead woman's neck, leaving her there for her family to take.

After the young man retrieved the body, taking it to a wagon, he gently placed the body in the wagon bed, and then he and the three children seated themselves on the driver's bench and rode off. I didn't see anyone walking around, so I took a chance and followed the wagon at a discreet distance until it stopped next to a barn near a small cabin. The man took his wife's body from the wagon bed and tenderly lowered it to the ground, placing it at the base of a tree.

While the children played quietly, he grabbed a shovel and began digging her grave. I saw and heard that he was sobbing with every shovelful until he had to go into the rectangle to dig it a little deeper. While he was doing this, I turned my attention to the children, seeing movement in the grass; it was a copperhead, rapidly approaching the children. Knowing I would have to expose myself in order to save one or more of the children from being bitten, I picked up a sizable tree branch and hurried toward the children The girl saw me and screamed, altering both the snake and her father. As the father climbed from the grave, the snake reared back and struck the little girl in the hand. Too late to stop that from happening, but able to toss it away from the other kids, I removed a pocketknife from my purse and, after holding the snake down with the forked portion of the branch, I knelt and cut its head off.

The father, his son, and the other daughter watched me as I hurried back to the little girl, slicing into the bite marks, and then sucking and spitting out the poison. Certain that I got it all and that the girl would be okay, I said to the father, "If there is a doctor in town, I'd take her in to make sure all the poison was removed from her blood." He just stood there and stared at me. Then he took my arm and guided me to his wife's body, removing her hood. I gasped when I saw her face; we were dead ringers except for the hair color.

"Who are you and how is it that you look exactly like my wife?" he inquired as tears flowed from his eyes.

"First, Sir, can I ask you where I am and what year this is?"

He appeared confused, but he answered. "You are in New Hartford, Connecticut and the year is 1663. Now, will you please answer my questions?"

I was shocked. A firm believer in time-travel, but never thinking I would ever do it myself, I answered by saying, "You won't believe this, but my name is Beverly Fair. I am twenty-five years old. I have traveled here from the future. The year I came from is 2001 and I came here from Fort Belvoir, Virginia, where I am a sergeant in the United States Army."

He contemplated what I had just said and after retrieving my purse and showing him my driver's license, he seemed to understand that I was indeed from the future. "May I help you bury your wife? I'll continue digging while you take your daughter to the doctor. Please!" I implored.

When he returned, I had finished digging the hole and he was shocked when he saw my mini dress and high heels. I had removed my bright yellow raincoat in order to have more mobility to use the shovel.

"You women in 2001 wear very little clothing," he said, smiling. "Jasmine will be fine thanks to you." He pulled her down from the wagon and then she raced to me, giving me a big hug as her father and her siblings laughed. When he saw the grave was ready, he and I lowered his wife's body into it. We covered her with a coarse piece of material that we wrapped around her body twice. He had used some twine to tie off the head and foot ends to keep dirt off her face. Using our hands and the shovel, we all contributed to filling in the grave. He then placed a cross as a headstone, and we walked into his cabin.

"He gave me a basin, a small piece of soap and a cloth to wash myself as best as I could in these primitive conditions. He had told me to look through his wife's things to see if something would fit me. I selected a long dress, forgoing the hideous undergarments and, when I joined the family at the supper table, I looked quite presentable.

"We talked for hours. Jacob, who was two, and Alice, a pretty four-year old, played while I talked. Jasmine was six and she seemed to understand many of the words I used, even though I had to explain their meanings sometimes. The father, Caleb, clung to every word.

"As time passed by, I became known to the townspeople as Caleb's cousin, here to take care of the children. We kept up that charade for over a year and then we fell in love. In order to continue our love affair, we had to move to another town, winding up in Norwich.

"We settled in and then we married, having two more children, boys. We named them James and Martin. Our lives were uncomplicated, and we bore the same struggles many people bore back in those days. This life continued for twelve years.

"Yesterday, we were out in a field picking blueberries to make a pie when I felt the tingle, much like I had felt all those years ago. I screamed 'No' at the top of my lungs and turned toward the kids and Caleb, and a moment later I was in a warehouse in 1930 before coming through the time tunnel to this place."

Nelson laughed at her reference to the old 1960's TV show, *The Time Tunnel.*

She took his hands in hers and quietly said, "Nelson, what happens to me now? I'm thirty-seven-years old, and I've been gone for a long time. How will I explain my age to my friends and family when I am sent home? Of course, my other question would be, will I ever be going home after my experiences and seeing this place?

Nelson Wainwright could only wonder.

18

Nelson stepped into the room of the second time--traveler who had fallen through the cracks. The director of the Time Travel Facility could not figure out how and why these two bouncers had been missed since they were somewhere, and somewhen else, utilizing the word Dan coined, for the past six years, while the TTF had been able to monitor all the other bouncers and TTIs

Simon Weisberg reclined in his lounge chair, watching TV when Nelson knocked on the door. "Come in," he said, pressing OFF on the remote.

Nelson entered the room and sat in a wingback chair, facing Weisberg. The man was fifty-one, born in Honolulu, Hawaii, and he had disappeared on March 7th, 1991, seven days after his twenty-ninth birthday.

"Hello, Simon. I've been going over your years of time- traveling and although I do want to hear about all your adventures, I am very curious about your trip to 1980 and what you wrote down during your initial interview. Was your statement a mistake?"

"No, Doctor Wainwright, it was no mistake. I killed John Lennon."

"Simon, John Lennon was gunned down on December 8th, 1980 by Mark David Chapman."

"Yes, I know, but I had the opportunity to stop him and I failed. I loved Lennon and I met him in 1976 when I was fourteen. Man, you talk about being star struck, I was hardly able to even say a word until he sat down beside me on the bench. My mom and my sister were inside a woman's clothing store when I saw John Lennon approaching. He was pushing a baby stroller with his son, Sean, inside, and there were no bodyguards or anyone else with him. Just a father and his son.

"He saw me staring at him and said, 'Hello young man, how are you today?' I could only stammer and stare at the legendary singer and after I said "Hello", I had no idea what to say next. He asked me if I would mind if he sat down and I just shook my head. John sat next to me after taking Sean from the stroller and placing him on his lap. He pointed to the clothing store entrance and smiled, 'Your mum inside there, young man? Do you have a name?' He extended his hand and said, 'I'm John Lennon, and this is my boy, Sean, but I'm quite sure you already know that.' I shook his hand and replied, 'I'm Simon Weisberg. It's a pleasure to meet you, Mr. Lennon.' Lennon smiled as we shook hands and said, 'Please call me John.' I nodded my head.

"We talked for several minutes, mostly about records and the magic of New York City. 'I want to live here till I die,' he said, with a wistful look on his face. He grew quiet for a minute, so I said, 'I've seen Paul, George, and Ringo play live, but I have never seen you on stage. Do you have a concert soon, John?'

"'No, Simon. I honestly don't know when I will perform live again.' He reached into his pocket and pulled out a roll of money. After peeling off a twenty, he handed it to me and said, 'There is a record store a couple of doors down from here. Rush down and get yourself any album you want, one of mine or one of The Beatles and bring it back here. I'll sign it for you.' 'John, that would be great, but my mom said I shouldn't move from this spot.' I sadly announced. He saw my expression and said, 'Tell ya what, mate. Sean and I will hurry down there and pick one up for you and when we come back, I'll sign it.'

'Thank you, John,' I replied as he hurried away.

"About a minute later, my mom and my sister came out from the store and told me they were ready to go. 'I can't,' I implored, 'John Lennon just went down to the record store to get an album for me. He's going to bring it back and sign it.' My sister laughed, 'John Lennon is getting *you* an album and he's going to sign it for you. Simon, you are just too funny.' She continued laughing, her head buried in her hands when Lennon and Sean returned with a copy of *Walls and Bridges.* She looked up at him and stammered, 'You're John Lennon!' 'That's right. You must be Simon's sister.' He turned to my mother and said, 'You have a fine boy here, Mrs. Weisberg.'

"The Lennons sat down next to me and after John signed the album and handed it to me, he said, 'Sean and I must go now. We have to get home and make dinner for Mother.'"

"With that said, he stood up, put Sean back in the stroller and walked down the street, signing autographs as he headed back to The Dakota."

"Thanks for sharing, Simon. I met Paul one time and got his autograph. He's a nice man too. Now back to the assassination. How did you kill John Lennon?"

19

In 2001, Dan was telling Ken and Arlen about where he really was on September 11th."Harry, Will, and I took my mini Winnie, a smaller version of a Winnebago and set up at our assigned camp site. The three of us had been going to this reunion for about ten years and became friends with many of the vets who attended. The actual reunion would not begin until Friday and then it would run through Sunday, but many veterans came early to set up and watch the small city grow. By Friday afternoon, there would be thousands of campers, pop-ups, tents, and other types of shelters housing over thirty-thousand vets, family members and supporters on an abandoned dirt airfield. For three days, this place would become Connecticut's seventeenth largest city.

"On 9/11, I awakened around seven thirty and a couple of minutes later, I began my run which would take me down the 'Main Street' of 'Veterans City' and out through the cornfields of rural western Connecticut for about three miles, and then I'd turned around to come back to prepare breakfast for Will and Harry. They liked sleeping in.

"Upon my return, I noticed that there was no music coming from any of the camp sites, which was highly unusual. I slowed when I saw a veteran take his flag down to half-staff. I strolled over to him and asked, "Why have you dropped your flag to half-staff?"

"'A plane crashed into the North Tower of the World Trade Center a couple of minutes ago and the building is burning like mad. Come on in and watch.' I quickly strode into his camper and sat down to watch what was going on. I saw smoke pouring from the tower and, on the ground, people were running like crazy trying to get away. I assumed it was a terror attack and when the second plane hit the South Tower, I knew for sure. Tears were rolling down my face as I watched the scenes unfold. Not too long after the attacks, people were jumping from the building, so as not to be burned to death. There was pandemonium. I thanked him for letting me watch and said, 'I better get back to my camper to see if my friends know what is going on.'

"Arriving at our camper, I hurried inside and saw that Harry and Will were watching the events on TV. My brother stood up and came over to hug me. 'Dan, do you think we will be getting into a war with whomever authorized these attacks?' 'Brother, I don't know, but I have a feeling I might get reactivated if we go to war. I hope I'm not too old for this shit again.' Harry and I were glued to the TV for most of the day after that.

"That evening a candlelight service was held in front of the big stage that had been set up for the bands that would play over the weekend. Seeing hundreds of candles held high was an inspiring sight and I believed that every vet holding a candle would be willing to sign back up to fight in the war on terror.

"Over the next several days, as tent city continued to grow, the mood was still very somber, but by Friday, when the site was open to all visitors, more of a party atmosphere had developed since everyone wanted to celebrate both Vietnam veterans and POW-MIA weekend, remembering those who had been captured and those who were still lost from past conflicts. We listened to the bands play our favorite songs from back in those days and we purchased a variety of items from all the vendors in the large tent.

"On Sunday, a church service was held, and I had never seen so many people stay for that in past years. We listened to a former army chaplain, heard the voices of a local choir singing meaningful contemporary Christian songs and participating in a mass communion. It was very moving.

"Before we left the grounds, several of the organizers took a collection for the victims and collected twenty thousand dollars and change. I was so proud to be an American and I always will be, Nelson."

20

Inside the TTF in 2013, Simon picked up a little notebook that had been lying on the end table next to his chair and he began to thumb through the pages.

"Simon, may I ask you what's written in that notebook?" Nelson asked.

"Certainly. I have always been prone to carry a little notebook with me, so I can jot down appointments and shopping lists since I tend to forget things. I had only purchased this one two days before I disappeared and in all my years of traveling, I have nearly filled all the pages with dates and places." He handed the book to Nelson. "As you can see, I employed very tiny letters and numbers having had no idea how long and to how many places I might travel. I realized I could go numerous places after only spending two days at my first stop in Michigan from May 2nd to May 4th in 1889 and then arriving in St. Louis, Missouri on April 22nd, 1972. I had been there for six weeks before moving on."

Impressed, Nelson handed the little notebook back and waited until Simon came to the entry about December 8th, 1980.

He had been counting his visits and he then said, "Ah, here it is. I arrived in New York City on my seventeenth adventure." He had written down numbers corresponding with each bounce in time. "I had been traveling for nine and a half years at this point..." Then it hit him. "Wow! I've been time-traveling for twenty-two years. Amazing!" He smiled. "I will have lots of stories to share with you as we go along."

Nelson smiled and nodded to him.

"Okay, after arriving in the city early in the morning, I immediately looked for something to show me the date I was now visiting. Seeing the date and remembering that it was the day that John Lennon was killed, I didn't want to see that happen. I couldn't recall Mark Chapman's movements that day, even after having read about them in the newspaper accounts, which would have been twenty years in the past, according to my *real* timeline. My stomach was rumbling, making me realize I hadn't eaten since early the previous morning, which was September

20th, 1967. I had been living in Brownsville Texas, since arriving there on March 18th, 1965. I worked at Hastings Cattle Feed Company where my job was as a delivery person. After having breakfast about 7 AM, I went to work. About five hours later, Hurricane Beulah made landfall nearby and my world turned to crap. High winds hit my truck, flipping it on its side, but I was able to get out of the cab and work my way to a nearby storm shelter. After the hurricane passed, those of us inside headed outside to see what we could do to help the nearby victims. Saving a family of four trapped on a roof after I found a rowboat, I got them off the roof and rowed the boat to dry land where they got off as I continued to travel on looking for more stranded people. I did that all day and finally collapsed inside a barn. When I woke up, I was in New York City on December 8th, 1980.

"I wanted to grab a bite to eat, but I really smelled bad, so I found a YMCA and grabbed a shower before heading back to the restaurant. All during breakfast, I tried to recall Chapman's movements during the day. I remembered that he had gone to the Dakota late that afternoon and had Lennon sign his copy of John's *Double Fantasy* album, so I figured I'd head over there to try to talk some reason into the man who was going to assassinate the former Beatle.

"After John and Yoko sped away in the limo, Chapman spoke briefly with a man and a woman, and then he slowly walked away. I caught up with him and said, 'Oh, man! You got John Lennon's autograph. That is so cool.' He smiled at me and nodded. 'John is very accessible to fans. Hang out at The Dakota and you'll probably be able to get him to sign something for you.' Then he laughed maniacally and added, 'I think he is going away tonight and won't be back for a long time, though.'

"Pushing him against the wall of a building, I said, 'I know where he is going tonight, and he's never coming back.' 'What do you know?' he retorted, with fear in his eyes. 'I know that you are going to kill him around 11 PM when he and Yoko return from the recording studio.' He shoved me off him and said, 'You're crazy, man! Why would I want to kill John Lennon? I'm a huge fan.'

"I motioned him to a nearby bench and asked him to sit with me. 'You are Mark David Chapman and you will kill John Lennon tonight. I know this because I am from the future and I'm here to stop you without harming you. Why do you want to do this, Mark?' He replied, 'I'm terribly angry with him because of many things he has said in the past and he needs to die for his sins.' 'Mark,' I said softly, placing my hands on his shoulders, 'If you kill him, you *will* spend the rest of your life in jail. Is that the way you want to be remembered?' He put his head on my shoulder and began to cry. 'I don't want to go to jail, but what am I going to do? Lennon is not the man he used to be, and he needs to be punished.' He paused for several moments and then looked me straight in the eyes. 'You are right, I can't kill him and spend the rest of my life in jail. Perhaps I should write a book?' 'That's a great idea, Mark. Please do not go to The Dakota tonight.' He stood up and we shook hands.

"I honestly believed he was not going to go to The Dakota, but closer to the time of the assassination, I got a bad feeling and rushed over there. My body was tingling, the sign that I would be time-traveling very shortly. I saw him watching John and Yoko as the two headed into the building and when I saw him raise his arm and point a gun at them, I managed to push him to the ground as I began to slide into the dark tunnel. I could still see him though. He rose into a combat stance and fired. I saw several bullets hit Lennon before I completely disappeared. I spent the next several years in time periods prior to 1980 and I didn't find out that Lennon had been killed until I arrived in 1983. I think that if I had not pushed him to the ground, he would have been standing and would have missed his target."

"That was quite a story, Simon, but I don't think you would have been able to stop the killing no matter what you would have done. There have been many instances when time-travelers have tried to change the past and they have always been blocked. In my mind, travelers are merely witnesses to history and here in the present, we are able to hear your stories."

"I'm a little tired right now, Nelson, but if you want stories, I have many to share with you whenever you are ready. You'll love the one about me having dinner with a former president of the United States.

"I'm looking forward to that very much, Simon." Nelson said, and with that, the director left the room to see what was going on in 2001.

21

That evening, the day before the world would change forever, Dan and Nelson met at Ellen's Stardust Diner in midtown Manhattan. The restaurant, which featured singing waiters and waitresses who were hoping to be discovered by a Broadway producer, was the brainchild of Ellen Hart, Miss Subways of March to April 1959. The Miss Subways program ran from 1941 to 1976. Each monthly winner's picture was placed on placards on the subways and viewed by nearly 6 million passengers daily.

In 1987, Ellen opened *Ellen's Stardust Diner*, featuring the singing waitstaff and some of the best diner food in the country. Over the years many Broadway and movie stars had dined here along with celebrities from other fields.

The diner was packed that evening and the waitstaff was in fine singing form while Dan and Nelson enjoyed their meals and a couple of cold beers. They were also treated to a table visit by the owner.

"Good evening, gentlemen. I'm Ellen Hart the owner of this diner. How were your meals?"

Dan and Nelson stood up and shook her hand. Nelson said, "Ellen you have a really great place and the food was awesome. I'm Nelson Wainwright and this is my friend, Daniel Rodin." Dan nodded in agreement.

"Thank you so much. What brings you men to the Big Apple? Or, do you live here?"

"I'm here because of some meetings and Dan just popped into town unexpectedly," Nelson offered.

She turned her attention to Dan. "Is this your first visit to New York?"

"No, I have visited here several times over my lifetime. I was last here about ten years ago when I was still in the army."

"Thank you for your service, Daniel. Were you an enlisted man or an officer? My guess would be that you were a high-ranking officer. It shows in your stature."

"Thank you, Ellen. Yes, I retired as a brigadier general in the infantry."

"Were you in Vietnam?"

"I was, along with my twin brother Harry, and a good friend, Will Jennings."

"Well, I am so glad you returned okay. I hope your brother and your friend are doing well, too."

"They are. Thanks."

"Ellen, I think it is really great that you support the young, upcoming entertainers who wait on us. They are so much fun to listen to."

"Thank you, Nelson. Many of our alumni have gone on to perform on Broadway and in movies. I hate to cut this conversation short, but I must chat with some more of my customers." As she walked away, Nelson and Dan noticed her talking to one of the waitstaff and pointing to their table.

The waiter strolled over and said, "Gentlemen, Ellen asked me to inform you that there will be no charge for your orders. If you would like more drinks, they will be taken care of as well. She has great respect for veterans, and I guess one or both of you are in that category. You certainly moved her."

Nelson and Dan saw Ellen looking toward them. They raised their glasses and nodded, getting a nod and a smile in return before she turned her attention to a young couple.

Dan said, "Are you looking forward to your meeting tomorrow?"

"That's what I want to talk to you about. I want to tell you what happened earlier and get your opinion." As they enjoyed their drink, Nelson said, "You appear much older than the last time I saw you. What's up with that?"

"Good question. A lot of people have been asking me that lately, and I honestly have no clue. I've been out in the sun a lot more in the past year or so, maybe my age lines have become more pronounced. I'm only six...fifty-two."

"Interesting slip of the tongue, Dan. Perhaps your mistake will be related to what I'm about to tell you."

Nelson told Dan about his meeting with Lawrence Delp and the offer that the man had made to him and three others. "What do you think?"

Dan laughed. "That was a hell of a story. I have no clue whether he is lying or not, but why would he want to take the four of you to Virginia on the strength of a lie. You'd all laugh at him and wonder why he would waste your time like that."

"I know. He sounded so sincere that I am really considering his offer. However, tomorrow's meeting could prove fruitful as well because I think I'm going to be offered a position that will pay me handsomely. You know how deeply I feel about time travel and to be one of the first to work on controlled time travel would be a dream come true."

"Well, I'm not going to disagree with you, Nelson, and you are the one who has to make the decision. Did you call Sara and talk to her about it?"

"Not yet, but I plan to very shortly." He kept staring at Dan, and he was convinced that something had happened to Dan to make him look so much older than when he last saw him, less than a year ago. He was going to climb out on a limb to see if he'd fall off. "Dan, are you a time traveler?"

Dan closed his eyes and nodded. Perhaps it was time to tell Nelson the truth.

Over another drink, Dan told Nelson all about his adventures in Gettysburg in 1863 and New York in 1930. He held back Nelson's current position not wanting to feed him more than he could chew.

"Why are you here in *this* time, Dan. Am I in trouble for something?"

Finally, Dan decided to tell him his fears. "Nelson, tomorrow at 8:46 a passenger plane is going to strike the North Tower, followed by a plane hitting the South Tower seventeen minutes later. At 9:37 the western side of the Pentagon will be hit by a passenger plane and at 10:03 a plane, probably bound for the White House or the Capitol, will be brought down when passengers break into the cockpit and force the plane to the ground."

For several minutes Nelson sat there stunned until saying, "Can we stop it?"

"I don't know who would believe us and *are* we supposed to change history. I am bucking the space time continuum I guess simply by being here. But, since you are alive in 2013, I think my mission is to not allow you to go to the North Tower tomorrow. You must go to Virginia and do what you are supposed to do and hopefully get me home."

Nelson forced a smile. So, I'm going to work in a time travel facility, but our actions will not allow us to change history? It still sounds farfetched, even to me, but you are right. I must continue on the path laid out for me. What are you going to do tomorrow?"

"Unless I'm shifted to somewhen else," creating a new word, Dan replied, "I'll help the victims of the attack as best as I can. I know how it's going to affect my younger self in Connecticut, and I have to tell you, I was a mess afterward for a long time."

After finishing their drinks, Nelson and Dan stepped outside into a sea of humanity.

22

In 2013, Nelson Wainwright had returned to Simon Weisberg's room. He had been watching the video of himself and Dan dining at Ellen's on September 10th, remembering how nice she was to them. Had they stayed another ten minutes, they would have seen Clarissa Fortuna enter the diner and sit at a table with several of New York City's dignitaries who had purchased copies of her book at a late afternoon signing.

He knocked on Simon's door and then entered. Simon was relaxing in his lounge chair watching *Wheel of Fortune.* He turned to the director of the TTF and said, "I love this program, especially solving the puzzles long before the contestants do. Perhaps someday I will apply to be a contestant. I guess you are ready to hear my story about Abraham Lincoln now.

"I would like that, Simon," he said as he took a seat in a chair facing the time-traveler.

"I had arrived in Springfield, Illinois on a ridiculously hot July 4th in 1837. The street was lined on both sides with people watching an Independence Day parade and I marveled at the patriotism of everyone in that city. After watching the entire parade, realizing I was very hungry, I strolled down the street to a restaurant, but when I sat down, I tried to find some money that would be good in this time period and I had none.

"A waitress came to my table to take my order and I told her I had no money to pay for a meal and could I please talk to the owner. I was shocked when she told me that she had been the owner of the place since her husband passed six months before. She told me that if I could help her in the kitchen by washing dishes, she would provide a meal for me for two hours of work. I agreed and after my chores were finished, she gave me a plate filled with meatloaf, mashed potatoes, and corn, plus a cup of extraordinarily strong coffee.

"After eating, I went back into the kitchen and washed more dishes, keeping at it until after the final customer for the day had gone home. I proceeded to put all the chairs on top of the tables upside down and then swept and mopped the floor.

"She thanked me and then asked me if I would like to work for her full time. I told her I would like that and asked her if she knew where I could get a room. 'I only arrived in town today and I have nowhere to stay.' She said, 'You can stay in a vacant room on the second floor and I will include your board with your daily pay for as long as you are with me.' I wound up staying for three months before I traveled again, but I had my biggest thrill on August 18th, when a tall, lanky lawyer sat down at a table. I had been looking out from the kitchen. When I saw Abraham Lincoln sitting there, I became a little star struck and came out to the dining room to introduce myself and shake his hand.

       "'Mr. Lincoln, it is such a pleasure to meet you,' I said. He replied, 'Thank you, Simon, and it is a pleasure meeting you as well. Have you had your supper yet?' I told him I had not. I asked my boss if I could take my dinner break now. She told me that would be fine, so I sat with the young lawyer and we discussed the events of the times. Out of the blue I asked him if the Southern states would ever consider breaking away from the United States. 'Simon, that is a particularly good question. I think we could have gotten into a Civil War, but President Jackson helped to avert that type of crisis. You see, South Carolina thought it was their right to nullify, or ignore laws that had been put in place years before. They also were dismayed about the taxes, actually federal tariffs, they had to pay on goods they were purchasing from outside the United States. He told the leadership of the state that federal law reigned over state law. Congress did cut the taxes a bit and a United States warship was seen in Charleston harbor, prepared to fire. Jackson finally got South Carolina to back down.' Lincoln took a sip of his coffee as I asked, 'What do you feel about the issue of slavery, which the Southern states back one hundred percent.' Lincoln thought for a moment and then replied, 'I do not think humans should own other humans and that issue must be addressed, hopefully sooner rather than later.' I nodded and then asked, 'What would you do if you were president?' He laughed. 'I am just a country lawyer, my friend. How could I possibly become president when there are so many more capable politicians out there who would probably be a fine president. No, Simon, I don't think I would ever become president, but thank you for asking; that was a nice compliment.' 'Well, I still think that you would be an amazing president and I hope if the time ever comes, you will run because I *know* you will win.' Lincoln chuckled as he chewed a forkful of roast beef and mashed potatoes. Then he looked into my eyes and inquired if I might be from the future to make such a statement. I lowered my voice and replied, 'I am, Mr. President. You will be elected in 1860 and guide our nation through a great civil war. You will free the slaves and put our country back together after the South is defeated. I cannot tell you any more than that, except to say that what I have just told you is the absolute truth.' I think he was in shock, but I needed to make certain that he would run.

"After I finished my dinner, I started to return to the kitchen to get back to work, feeling the tingle course through my body. I opened the kitchen door and as I stepped through, I disappeared, winding up at Woodstock in 1969."

"Simon, thank you for sharing. Perhaps you did guide Lincoln toward the White House and for that I thank you. Now, I have to get back to my other work, but I hope to speak with you again in the next day or so." He walked back to his office and sat down hard, wondering if Simon did change the future. Perhaps Lincoln would never have run. Could time-travelers have altered the future into the one we know today? Were they sent back to ensure that our present history would remain what it is? There were too many questions and he wondered if he would ever get the answers. He still had to interview the remaining bouncers to see what changes they could have made to create our present timeline.

September 11th, 2001/July 8th, 2013

1

Steve Williamson, a driver for Lehigh Valley Bus, had been taking people to Wall Street for nine years without incident. On 9/11, he parked his bus two blocks from the World Trade Center where his riders dismounted. A handful of his passengers raced toward the Twin Towers and Steve smiled, figuring they were running late for a meeting.

Once his riders were clear of the bus, Steve quickly went into a nearby restaurant to grab a cup of coffee before taking the vehicle to the all-day parking lot for busses. He had just unlocked the door when he heard a tremendous boom and when he looked toward the North Tower, he saw it in flames with black smoke drifting upward. Thinking a plane had somehow gotten off course and hit the structure, he wasn't overly concerned until he saw numerous NYPD cars heading to the building, followed by several fire trucks.

He calmly sipped his coffee, watching the scene develop when about fifteen minutes later, a second plane hit the South Tower. Steve now knew that this was a terror attack on the city and the United States. He raced toward the Twin Towers, just wanting to do something besides standing there staring at the conflagration. As he closed in on the scene, a piece of concrete as big as a basketball, hurtled toward him and had he not veered to the left, he would probably have been killed.

Seeing about ten wounded people coming out from the buildings, he raced toward them. Steve had been a medic in the army for five years and he was ready to care for these people, even though he had no bandages or anything to clean their wounds. He took off his uniform shirt and his t-shirt and began tearing pieces from them to use as dressings.

2

Moments after Steve stepped out from the restaurant, Dan and Nelson walked out too. It was less than a minute from impact of the first plane and they turned toward the World Trade Center. They heard the plane when the hijackers increased power as they approached the building shortly before the crash. The sound of the plane hitting the building assailed their ears and then they saw the smoke and flames coming from the North Tower. On the ground there was mass confusion as residents and visitors had no idea what was happening. Once the realization of a plane hitting the World Trade Center sank in, many of them began to run away from the impending danger while some raced toward it. Dan and Nelson both saw a bus driver calmly looking toward the WTC, drinking his coffee until the second plane hit sixteen minutes later. They saw him race toward the towers and then kneel to help some wounded people.

Dan and Nelson also hurried to the scene, giving comfort and first aid as best as possible to the injured people lying or walking on the street and the sidewalk. Dan looked up and saw a person jump from the North Tower, so as not to be burned to death. It was hard for him to relive these scenes again as a man from the future, while his younger self was viewing them from the reunion site. Nelson found a woman with a large gash in her leg. He took off his suit coat and ripped off his shirt, tearing strips to bind her wound and the wounds of others he would find. Debris began to pelt them. When the towers would fall in less than an hour, the impending dust storm would create a massive cloud, creating difficulty to breathe.

3

Steve continued methodically providing first aid and comfort to as many people as he could. He came upon an older woman who appeared to have a dislocated shoulder. He knew what to do because he had reset a couple of shoulders during his time in the army, but he was afraid because of her age. "Ma'am," he said, "You have a dislocated shoulder and I'm going to try to reset it. It may hurt but I don't know how long it might be before they will be able to get you professional medical treatment. Is it okay if I do this for you?"

"Yes, son, please do your best. It hurts like hell and I don't know how long I will be able to put up with the pain."

"Okay, first I want to have you sit up and then I can get to work," Steve said, smiling.

The woman sat up and looked at her benefactor who was kneeling beside her. As he massaged her shoulder she asked, "What is your name, young man?"

"I'm Steve Williamson. Now relax while I set this shoulder."

He massaged her shoulder trying to get the muscles to relax and when he felt they were loosened enough, he took her arm and began moving it out away from her body to the side until he heard the pop of the shoulder going back into place. He took off his belt and created a sling to keep the arm and shoulder immobile until paramedics would be able to work on her and get her better treatment. "How does that feel now, ma'am?"

"Oh, Steve, it feels so much better. Thank you."

He stood up, ready to move on to the next person in need. "You're welcome, ma'am."

Just before he walked away, she called out, "I'm Clarissa Fortuna and thanks again."

Three days later, Steve would receive a signed copy of Clarissa's book.

4

In 2013, Nelson watched the unfolding scenes in awe. He was impressed with Steve's medical skills, considering he had little to work with in medicinal products, only his first aid kit that he retrieved from the bus before running toward the burning buildings. He was a marvel to watch.

He had Googled Steve only minutes ago and found that he had retired from Lehigh Valley Bus just two months ago.

Nelson also watched Dan as he worked on several injured people, not knowing what effect his intrusion into the past would do to the timeline. There was so much he did not know about time-travel and perhaps everything that had been written about the subject could be wrong. He still had to listen to a lot of travelers and knowing that he had left the scene in 2001 after treating some injured people, there was really nothing that could keep him glued to the video screen at this time. He strolled to the room of a traveler named James Gillespie.

5

Thirty-two-year-old James Gillespie disappeared in 2000. He was working at his job as a railroad conductor and as he was preparing to enter a car after exiting one, he vanished, unseen by anyone else. When the engineer found out that he was gone, a search had begun covering all the ground the train had traveled since the last time he had been seen about an hour before he was reported missing.

Nelson knocked on his door and after hearing 'Come in,' he stepped inside. "Good morning, Mr. Gillespie, how are you today?" he inquired as he took a seat.

James Gillespie was lying in bed with a cast on his leg. He had broken it during his final time-traveling experience before arriving at the warehouse in 1930. A New York City doctor had reset it and put it in a cast only hours before he passed through the thin green membrane separating 1930 from 2013. He was drinking a Diet Coke and eating a ham and cheese sandwich while watching an old movie on TV. "I'm fine, Dr. Wainwright, except for the damn itching in my leg. I don't know what they used to make my cast, but it certainly was not as well made as the one I had to wear on my wrist in 1999 when I fractured it."

"Where and when did you break it, James, if I may? Please call me Nelson."

"You may, Nelson. Thanks. I had been in 1350 for about six months when it happened. I was working for a doctor and my job was to make certain that all of his ointments and medical supplies were kept in order on a high shelf above his medical books and other reading materials. In order to take items down or replace them, I had to climb six rungs on a makeshift ladder, which was not the sturdiest one I have ever employed.

"I was on the top rung getting two jars of ointments for the doctor when the rung broke in half and I tumbled to the floor. My left foot hit the floor and then twisted on the uneven surface. I heard a crack and was almost certain that I had broken my fibula. After the initial pain, it didn't hurt too much, but the doctor wanted to take care of me as quickly as possible. He called for a couple of strong men to come inside. They lifted me onto the examination slash surgical table and when the doctor lifted my robe, he saw the break and the torn skin.

"I was given a piece of leather to place between my teeth to lessen the noise I was probably going to make as the doctor and one of the men worked on setting the break, which was not the best way in twenty first century medicine, but in 1350, it was the best they could do. After playing around with my leg for a long time, I finally heard a snap as the bone was set. The doctor applied a black, foul smelling ointment to the open wound and then they placed wooden splints around my leg and tied them tightly with several rope bindings, to hold the reset bone in place.

"A wooden cast, which they called a cradle, was built around my leg and I was handed a pair of crude crutches and sent on my way. I hobbled to my small hut and fell onto my bed. I felt that I was now sporting a bit of a fever but gutted it out over the next couple of days before hobbling back to see the doctor and to try to do whatever work I could do. I had to earn some money to keep myself alive until I would feel that welcome tingle and be sent somewhere else. I was hoping that I would be propelled into the future where the medical community would be able to repair my leg. I really was not looking forward to the prospect of limping around for the rest of my life.

"Fortunately, I only remained in 1350 for ten more days before arriving at the warehouse yesterday. I know I am scheduled for surgery tomorrow to have my broken fibula repaired properly and the doctor who examined me earlier said that after they finished, I would be fine after a couple of weeks. What will happen to me after that, Nelson? In real time, I have been gone for thirteen years. I'm now forty-five; my kids have grown up without me around. My son is nineteen and my daughter is twenty-one. Can you tell me what they are doing? Have I been declared dead and has my wife moved on with her life? I need these questions answered, Nelson or I fear I will go out of my mind. During my travels I have seen many things that I never want to see again. I rode with Custer, and I spent two horrific weeks on Iwo Jima. I survived a trip on the Mayflower, and I came out of the great Chicago fire without any harm having been done. Nelson, I want my life back, but I don't think I will ever get it, will I?"

Nelson sat there in a state of shock after James' tirade, and although he knew what happened to the man's family-they were killed by a drunk driver four years ago-he could not give him any answers at the moment.

6

Feverishly working on the injured and dazed, Nelson looked at his watch. He, Dan, and Steve, along with several paramedics, and off duty nurses, had been at it for forty minutes. It was now 10:57 and the South Tower would begin to collapse in two minutes. Afterwards, there would be too much smoke, dust, and debris to continue minor first aid. Dan looked over to Nelson and gave him the two-minute warning signal with his fingers. Nelson nodded but he continued to assist a paramedic who was treating a stomach wound.

When the first tower fell, screams filled the surrounding area, and a cloud rolled out of the debris, filled with both harmless papers and lethal bits of metal as concrete pelted the men and women who were still trying to offer comfort to the injured. People who had gotten closer to the buildings, watching the horror unfold, had now turned around and started to run toward the good Samaritans tending to twenty to twenty-five injured people. Dan got bowled over by a middle-aged man carrying a briefcase, who then stumbled himself. The man just picked himself up and with no regard to Dan, continued running away from the scene.

Dan went back to work giving aid and comfort to the injured, remembering what he was doing at this exact moment in Connecticut. He, Harry, and Will were watching the news and when the South Tower collapsed, he recalled that tears came to his eyes as he tried to imagine what it could have been like being trapped inside the building. Before the collapse, the cameras panned to the buildings where he watched people on fire throwing themselves from the structures, not wanting to burn to death. Their eyes were glued to the scenes unfolding and watching the pandemonium on the ground at times was unbearable. Less than a half hour later, the North Tower collapsed, creating more smoke, dust, and debris. The loss of life was unfathomable to the Vietnam veterans and they cried unabashedly.

Dan and Nelson continued their tasks well into the afternoon and finally, when everyone had been treated and sent to hospitals or to their homes, the two friends walked away, both needing a strong drink and some food. They would spend three hours talking about what had just occurred and what was to come. Dan was hesitant about telling Nelson anything more about the future, so he decided the less said the better.

7

In 2013, after watching Dan and his younger self discuss the day's events, Nelson found himself shaking, reliving all of those moments again. He had a job to do, and now it was time to interview two more travelers.

Alyssa Collins, a sixty-two-year-old real estate agent in Hyannis, Massachusetts, had disappeared in 1975. She had been loading the back of her station wagon after getting two weeks-worth of groceries at Shaw's. She had twelve large shopping bags along with a couple of cases of soda to load. Jerome Yanger, a seventeen-year old senior at Barnstable High School had been pushing carts back to the store from the parking lot when he saw Alyssa struggling with her purchases. He came over to help her and when Alyssa felt the tingle, she felt herself being pulled away and screamed, 'Jerome, please help me.' Jerome saw that she was being lifted off the ground and he grabbed her around the legs to pull her back to earth. Seconds later, they were both gone. Surprisingly, nobody had seen what happened and their disappearances were not noticed until the store manager went looking for Jerome.

Although they each had their own rooms, Nelson requested that they be together for the interview. He had them escorted to a small lounge, generally reserved for high government officials who were aware of the existence of the TTF. He stepped inside the room and saw Alyssa and Jerome in animated discussion. Nelson had discovered that during the period of time they were in the warehouse in 1930, they didn't recognize each other, twenty-eight years having passed by.

"Hello, you two. I hope I have given you enough time to catch up a little and discuss your experiences. You are the only travelers we have found to have bounced in tandem, and I understand from preliminary reports that you both went your separate ways and were only reunited yesterday."

They nodded and Jerome gave Alyssa a sign that she should begin.

"Yes, that's true," she said. "I can still remember it like it was yesterday. It felt like I was getting sucked into space and I cried out for help. Jerome grabbed me around the legs, and we disappeared. I continued to feel him holding me until I found myself on a ship in the Atlantic Ocean. The ship turned out to be a cruise ship, and I had no idea exactly where I was. I arrived at night when most people were asleep, so my instant appearance didn't cause any panic. I was dressed appropriately, although my clothes were a little dated, and before going grocery shopping, I had cashed my check. I had nearly five-hundred dollars in cash in my purse, which was good because I didn't know how long I would be at sea without a room.

"I curled up on a lounge chair by the pool. The night was extremely warm, so I was okay without any kind of blanket or sheet, and I fell asleep quickly. I awakened to the scents of coffee and food being cooked. Realizing I hadn't eaten in probably twelve hours, I headed into the breakfast buffet and simply pigged out. I knew I wouldn't have to worry about paying for meals as long as I was on the ship, so that was a good thing." She laughed at the thought, also getting chuckles from Nelson and Jerome.

"Sometime before I awakened, we had docked and I had hoped it was somewhere in the United States because I didn't have a passport, and I couldn't fathom the thought of sleeping on a lounge chair for another night. After breakfast, I looked to see where we were, but before finding a vantage point, I heard a young man say, 'So what shall we do during our six hours in Boston.' I can't tell you how happy I was for that because I had a great college friend living in the city and she had opened her own real estate business immediately after getting her license the summer after we graduated. The woman was quite ballsy for the times and I applauded her determination to be one of the youngest million-dollar real estate agents in the country.

"I was excited with the prospect of seeing her until I saw a calendar and found out that it was July 19th, 1994. She'd be forty-three and I was still twenty-four. There would be no way that I could explain that I looked the same as I did back in the day, while she had aged almost twenty years. I thought that perhaps she wouldn't even be in the real estate business anymore. She was always reaching for the stars and I knew that she had also wanted to be a famous singer, another one of her dreams. I had to go on shore and at least get a new outfit that would pass scrutiny. I also knew I would have to budget carefully, not knowing how long I would be there in that time.

"At a newspaper machine, I grabbed a copy just to see what was going on in the city and to see if I could find anything that would help me understand what had transpired in the past nineteen years. As I raced through it, turning each page after scanning the headlines, I found that Nick Price had won the British Open, and Crayola announced the introduction of scented crayons, as well as a lot of local news that didn't do much for me. I decided that if I went to a library, perhaps I could find out a lot about what had occurred during the years I totally missed out on, and I guess I will never get back." She stared at Nelson for conformation, but he only shrugged his shoulders, saying, 'Please continue.'

"The saddest part of my time-travels was when I returned home three years after disappearing. Prior to that, I spent a couple of years in Bangor, Maine, beginning on VJ Day, August 14th, 1945. World War II had ended about a week after we dropped two atomic bombs, forcing the Japanese to surrender.

"When I found myself back in Hyannis, twenty-eight years after my first disappearance, the visit was bittersweet. A lot of things had changed. Many businesses had closed up and new ones opened. After walking through town for about an hour, I decided to visit the Oak Neck Cemetery. My dad had passed away when I was sixteen and I had been so upset that, after his funeral, I never visited his grave again. He had been killed when an intruder walked into his store just before Dad was ready to close for the day. The man robbed him of all his money and then killed him for absolutely no reason. I've hated guns since that day too." She took a few moments to compose herself after telling that story.

When she recovered, she said, "Anyway, when I found Dad's grave, I was shocked to see that my brother had passed away in 1997. When he came home from Vietnam in 1971, he was not the same person he had been in 1970. He had seen a lot of combat and won a Silver Star, a Bronze Star, and he was awarded three Purple Hearts for his wounds. He couldn't keep a job and the last time I saw him was in 1973. He left Hyannis that year, but after finding his obituary in the newspaper on microfilm, I found out that he had returned in 1977. He told no one where he had been or what he had done while he was gone. My dad had served in combat during World War II and Korea and he was always troubled after two wars. They found Rick's body next to Dad's headstone. He had killed himself." She began to cry, and it took several minutes for Jerome and Nelson to settle her down. When she was okay again, she asked if she could take a break and went back to her room.

8

After parting company in 2001, Nelson and Dan went their separate ways.

Dan returned to his hotel room and stood by the window where last night he stared at the towers for a long time; tonight, they were gone and he just felt terrible that he could not stop the planes from crashing into the buildings. Yesterday he toyed with the idea of going to a National Guard center to steal a bazooka or a hand-held rocket launcher and then head to the roof of the North Tower to await the approaching plane and shoot it down. If he would be able to get two weapons, he thought he might possibly have been able to shoot both planes down, hopefully over water before they hit. Of course, he realized that he was not here to change history, except perhaps to save Nelson's life today.

As he continued to focus on the empty space a couple of blocks away, something on the outside sill caught his attention and he looked down to see what it was. He burst into tears and then he opened the window, picking the item up with a clean towel. It was a female left hand with an engagement ring and a wedding ring on the second finger.

He wrapped it and took it to the nearest police station, hoping that they might be able to find out whose hand and rings they now had in their possession. He knew Nelson would be watching him in 2013, so he quietly said, "Nelson, I hope you can find out whose hand and rings these were. If the cops can't do it, perhaps 2013 technology will be able to find out." He stopped in at the nearest bar and sat down.

9

Moments before Nelson opened the door to the interview room, his iPhone rang. He answered it and smiled. His staff had found the owner. They were going to notify NYPD so the police could return the rings to the family. Of course, a story would have to be concocted to not let the police know about the TTF.

He stepped into the room and asked Alyssa if she was okay. She nodded. Before she had returned to her room, she asked Nelson not to have Jerome tell his story because she wanted to hear it, too. They all agreed to a one-hour break.

Nelson said, "Jerome, are you ready to share your story?"

He smiled, nodded, and then began.

"Like Alyssa, I also found myself on a ship. During the time it took to get from Hyannis to this place was probably less than a minute and I clung tight to her, but I felt a separate pull and saw her drift away, I felt a sting on my neck when I arrived and realized that it was a spark from the coal fires that were being fed by several strong looking men. They were all sweaty because the heat that was escaping from the open metal doors was excruciating. They were so busy that nobody paid any attention to me. I looked around and saw that I was in the boiler room of an exceptionally large ship and I soon began to believe that I had traveled back in time to the days of steam ships.

"I left the boiler room and began to work my way through empty corridors, passing by locked doors. I had attempted several, trying to get my bearings and, hopefully to find someone who could tell me where I was. I had no success, but I finally arrived at a staircase and I climbed the stairs until I finally made it to the upper deck where I could see the ocean. I looked around and when I saw the four stacks, I knew I was on the Titanic, but I didn't know how long I would have until the ship would sink. I was really scared of dying forty-six years before I would be born.

"As I walked aft, toward the rear of the ship, I really felt the biting cold. I was wearing jeans, a Boston Red Sox T-shirt, a black baseball cap and my white apron. I had on Keds sneakers and that was it. Remember, Alyssa and I disappeared during one of the hottest spells on the Cape that year. Anyway, I finally arrived at the at the stern and I could see the Irish coast in the distance. The Titanic had left there around 1:30 PM on April 11th, and it wouldn't hit the iceberg for another eighty-two hours. My knowledge was terrific because I had written a book report on the Titanic last year in school. Can you even imagine what it would be like knowing you probably only had less than eighty-two hours to live?

"I stood there, watching us race away from land when a man came to the railing and stood beside me. I looked at him and saw he was dressed to the nines, concluding that he was probably one of the wealthy first class passengers, not that it would mean anything to him in a noticeably short period. He would drown, a horrible death, and all the money in the world would not change that ending.

"He noticed my apron and inquired if I was a kitchen worker. I told him I was, and he said, 'I don't think you should be up on this deck, young man. Perhaps if you take your apron off, nobody else will notice.' He stared at my T-shirt and asked if the Red Sox had changed the logo on their team shirts. 'No,' I laughed. 'This is the 1975 T-shirt. I just bought it last week in Hyannis.' I had momentarily forgotten where and when I was and the shocked look on his face revealed my faux pas Then he laughed and said, 'You are quite the jokester, young man. 1975 when it is only 1912.' Then he became stoic and said, 'Unless you are from the future?'

"I wondered if he had any pull with the captain, so I said, 'Yes, I am. I arrived on this ship after being whisked away from my job as a grocery store clerk in Hyannis,

Massachusetts. I have to tell you that this ship will hit an iceberg at 11:40 PM on April 14th and over fifteen hundred people will die. He was momentarily stunned but recovered quickly. He smiled and said, 'Since you are from the future, I am certain you have no room. In the time we have left, I want to hear about everything I am going to miss, and even beyond that. I want to learn everything you know about the future. First, we must get you to the ship's store where I can purchase an appropriate outfit or two for you and you will, of course, stay in my room. I have a suite and there is more than enough space for an extra person. We will have four sumptuous suppers before we die, and we will drink the finest wines I can purchase.'

"After donning a new three-piece suit and black wingtip shoes, I looked more like a 1912 passenger than a 1975-time-traveler. I was at my benefactor's side from that moment until after the ship hit the iceberg. Neither of us had been able to sleep and we wanted to be on the Lido deck when we crashed into the berg, hoping to stay alive a little bit longer. When the ship hit, he grew terribly afraid and ran away from me. I tried to find him, but I had no luck.

"I raced toward the stern, knowing that the rear end would be the last to go. As the ship began to sink, I found myself going uphill and when the first smokestack broke apart, the noise was incredible. Reaching the stern", I tied myself to the railing with a rope I had found on the way to the rear of the ship.

"The ship was tilted at more than a forty-five-degree angle, and suddenly the screeching sound of tearing metal, and the cracking of heavy wood, assaulted my ears. The ship had broken in half and, after that occurred, the back of the ship fell back down into the sea, creating a great plume of water that soaked me to the skin. It was so frigid that I thought I might freeze to death before I drowned.

"Suddenly the Titanic once again rose out of the water and as it began its downward trek, it was nearly standing straight up. I quickly untied myself, hoping that I would be able to survive the pull of the ship as it began its trip to the bottom of the ocean. As soon as I felt myself slide under water, I swam as hard as I had ever swum in my life and I popped above the surface staring at a lifeboat about fifty yards away. With each stroke, I thought my body was going to give up the fight, but I kept going, finally reaching the boat, and being pulled inside.

"My body temperature had dropped significantly, but the survivors wrapped me with jackets and blankets and even covered me with their bodies until my body heat returned. I knew I would live, and I thought that perhaps a time-traveler could not die before he or she was even born. Sometime during the night, when everyone had fallen asleep, I disappeared.

10

In 2001, after Dan sat down at the bar, a man, and a woman, both in business clothes, sat down next to him. Their suits were covered with dust and scraps of paper, and the man had a long scratch on his left cheek. The woman's skirt was torn from hem to mid-thigh, and Dan saw that her thigh was covered with a four-inch all-around bandage. He asked them if they had been in the towers.
When they nodded, he got the bartender's attention and bought them drinks.

Dan asked them, 'How the hell did you get out?"

The woman, after downing her cocktail in one long swallow, replied, "Merrill and I were truly fortunate to come out of there alive. We have been having an affair for three years, both of us are married, and after having sex on his desk, we got dressed and headed down to my office five floors below. As we were walking down the steps, I heard the plane tearing into the building and then I felt the stairs moving back and forth. I could vaguely hear screaming from above and I honestly thought I was going to die that day."

Merrill said, "Sandee and I are in love and as we have been sitting here drinking and thinking about how and why we survived, we've decided to tell our spouses about our affair and that we both wish to get divorces so we can be together. It may not be right because we are Christians, but for what other reason would God save us?"

Dan thought for a moment and replied, "Perhaps He wanted you both to survive for your families. I'm not going to judge either of you because I don't know what kind of lives you have with your spouses. If you both have kids, you should really think about what you are going to tell them. I had a friend who had left his wife when his kids were adults. They didn't talk to my friend for years until my friend was in a bad automobile accident and nearly died. For about five years now, my friend and his kids have become awfully close. I just think you guys should talk this over a little more, maybe even sleep on it, before you talk to your spouses. We have all been under a tremendous amount of stress today and you might need a little time to see things differently."

The three of them talked for about an hour, all of them having drunk too much. Sandee and Merrill did not even experience any shock when Dan vanished in front of their eyes.

11

Nine hours had passed, but Dan was nowhere to be found. Nelson was afraid that he had possibly disintegrated in a wormhole and would never return, and he couldn't fathom that his friend might be gone forever.

However, he still had a job to do and he had many interviews to complete. Although his heart was not in it, he was hoping that the stories he was about to hear might offer more insight to the experience of being a time traveler. He stepped into an interview room.

The Time-Travelers

Ellen Wakley
September 14th, 1985 to July 8th, 2013

1

"I remember my time travel experience well; it's hard to forget disappearing from a lucrative modeling gig, especially being naked.

"Even when I was a kid, I took off my clothes as often as I could. I loved when I was able to strip and take a shower after gym class. My body had developed more quickly than my schoolmates and I couldn't help but watch many of the girls ogle me as I washed. At twelve, my breasts were already an impressive size 32, along with a slim waist, long legs, and a tuft of pubic hair that was dark brown, I was the most physically mature girl in my school, perhaps in my town. I had a pretty face, dark brown, long, wavy hair, brown eyes and classic features that made even boys a couple of years older go apeshit. I must admit, I flaunted my good looks as often as I could.

"I lost my virginity when I was fifteen during summer vacation and, although there have been times I regretted having sex that early, I enjoyed it as much as, or more than, anything else I did. My parents were very liberal, but they did punish me for my sexual adventures more than one time. I guess I was the black ewe of the family. My sister remained a virgin until she married at twenty-two, and she was almost as attractive as I was. When I had lost my virginity, I told her about it, since she was three years older, and she hung on every descriptive word I used to verbally act out the sex. We had shared a bedroom and as I told her,

I saw her hand slide beneath her blanket. That made me smile, knowing I could tell a story and have someone get that excited, especially a sister.

"By the time I turned twenty-one, I had had too many men to count, but I was always careful to not get pregnant. I had lived in a small town, Tarryville, in Montana, and there wasn't much for a girl in the way of jobs, so I decided to move to New York City. For three years I did some straight modeling and then one day I was approached by an artist who wanted to paint me nude. He offered me two-thousand dollars for the job, telling me it would take about a week. I figured he would also want sex, and I had no problem with that.

"During the fifth session, he had stepped out from the room to get some more paint and as I waited, I felt a chill like the temperature had fallen below freezing, I covered myself with my arms and crossed my legs to ward off the cold when my body began to tingle as though a thousand volts of electricity were passing through it. I saw the door open and the artist stepped into the room. The last thing I saw was him dropping the paints and I could hear him cry out as I totally disappeared."

2

"All these years later, I can still feel the pull from the present to the past and although it was scary, I was looking forward to seeing where I would wind up. The ride, for lack of a better term, took a couple of minutes as I recollect, and when I arrived at my destination, I tripped on some rocks, breaking my right ankle and my left elbow. I had looked at myself and saw I was still naked, obviously, and I was in a field that was being plowed. The air was crisp, and it didn't take long for a chill to seep into my body. I managed to sit, which was not great considering my lack of clothes, so I tried to stand up, but my ankle hurt like hell. Soon, a man pulling a horse drawn plow noticed me and I think he was quite taken aback, seeing a nude woman in his field. I yelled, 'Help, help me please.'

"He let go of the reins and dropped the plow. It took him about a minute to reach me and he couldn't hide his embarrassment from me. 'Miss, what happened? How did you get here? Where are your clothes.'

"I said, 'It's a long story, mister, but first I would like to get my ankle and elbow tended to. I'm certain they are both broken.'

'Wait here a minute, 'he replied.

"He raced back to his horse, disconnected the plow, and then led the beautiful steed toward me. I wondered how he was going to get both of us up on the horse's back, but it turned out to be quite easy. He jumped up on the mare and grabbed my hand, pulling me up behind him. As we rode toward his farmhouse, I could tell he was quite uncomfortable with my breasts pressing into his back. His shirt was sweat soaked from working the field and as we rode, the sweat evaporated and the coarse material rubbed against my nipples. Of course, the inevitable happened and he tried to wriggle forward a little to not feel them in his back.

"I had my arms wrapped around his waist so I could stay on the horse. I had ridden some when I was a kid, but never bareback and I did have some difficulty staying on the mare.

"When we arrived at his farmhouse, he dismounted and then pulled me down, cradling me in his arms. We went inside and I sat on a chair. He went into the bedroom and came out with a dress, a couple of sizes too large, but that was okay. I was beginning to get a little uncomfortable with the situation as well.

"He said, 'I'm going to go to the barn and hitch Sarah to the wagon and then we're going to go into town to see the doc. He should be able to fix you up today and at least ease your pain.'

"I nodded, but he had already turned and walked out the door. During the time he was gone I looked around the farmhouse to see if I could get a clue to the time period I was now in and beside the potbellied stove, I saw a stack of newspapers. I stood up and hobbled to them, grabbing the top one and returning to the chair.

"The newspaper was called *Stiles Weekly,* and the issue was dated Saturday, April 15th, 1893. Now I knew that I was in Stiles, Oklahoma at a young farmer's place. I assumed that his wife, or mother, was no longer with him, but he hadn't tossed her clothing. Perhaps the death, or whatever happened was recent.

"The farmer retuned to the house after driving the wagon close to the door. He stepped inside and carried me to the wagon. He was going to have me lay in the wagon bed for the ride to town, but I insisted that I felt well enough to ride on the seat beside him.

"This was the beginning of an adventure that was going to turn my life completely around."

3

"As we traveled the rutted road into town, my ankle and elbow were jolted with pain at each bump in the road, and over the nearly twenty-mile trip, there were many.

"He hadn't said a word to me from the moment we left his farm and I figured we had been on the road for about a half an hour. The silence was making me crazy.

Finally, I said, nearly as a shout, 'I want to thank you for what you are doing for me, sir. My name is Ellen Wakley.' Nothing from him in return. 'Are we still on your property, or are we riding through public land?' I was now thinking he owned the word stubborn when he didn't reply, but I was not about to give up. I was not built that way. 'Would you at least tell me your name? Why in the hell are you giving me the cold shoulder, Mister?'

"He pulled back on the reins and stopped the wagon, staring at me with the coldest look I had ever seen in my life. 'Do not cuss in my presence, young lady. In these parts we have civil tongues and the only place one will hear language like that is in the local saloon. If you want to speak to me in that tone, I will drop you off there instead of at the doctor's office. The owner could probably find suitable employment for a woman who uses such language. But I will tell you my name. It is Silas Gaines. Now, if you would please let me drive, we'll get to town and get you taken care of.'

"I was left speechless for a few moments, but I was not going to sit in silence for however long it was going to take to get to town. However, I figured that if I were going to get him to converse with me, I would have to try a different tact. 'I apologize, Mr. Gaines. I have recently moved here from New York City, and I fear that too many of us speak like that. I was just a little angry that you would not answer my questions. I realize that my appearance has caused you much concern, and I do wish I could tell you why you found me naked, but I am certain you would never believe me.'

"I was hoping for a response, but Mr. Gaines remained stoic and simply drove the wagon. About five minutes later, he finally responded. 'In my studies, I have learned that not everything has a plausible explanation unless one believes in God, and that He does indeed work in mysterious ways. I do not know why He sent you to my farm, unclothed, but if you do tell me how you arrived here, perhaps I can accept that. My faith is extraordinarily strong, and your presence might be part of God's plan for me. I will listen to whatever you have to tell me.'

"Without giving him dates, I capsulized my life story using just the basic elements and after a few minutes I ended by saying, 'I was posing nude for a young artist and I felt a tingle throughout my entire body. I was disappearing in front of him and the next thing I knew I was in your field.' When he looked toward me, I added, 'The date that occurred was September 14th, 1985, ninety-two years from now.

"He stopped the wagon and said, 'Miss Wakley, please excuse me for a few minutes. I need to take a walk to digest everything you just told me.' Without another word, he strolled away from the wagon."

4

"When he returned to the wagon ten minutes later and climbed aboard, he said, 'Your story is awfully hard to accept, but I cannot think of a logical answer. From the spot in my field where I found you, I have a three-hundred-and-sixty-degree view of the landscape, which probably reaches out over a mile. Less than two minutes before I heard you call out and came to you, I had stopped for a drink of water and I swept the land with my eyes for that entire three-hundred-and-sixty-degrees, and you were not to be seen. If your story is true, I will want you to stay with me at my farm. You will be able to teach me many things, Ellen, if I may call you by your Christian name.

"'You may, and I will tell you whatever I can without trying to change the future as I know it. I have always been fascinated with the concept of time-travel, and I have devoured many books on the subject. We also have visual time-travel offerings, which we call television and movies. In fact, only two months ago in my time, a time travel movie was released titled *Back To The Future.* Silas, I will tell you many things that will rattle your brain, but everything I tell you will be the absolute truth.'

5

"After my ankle and elbow were repaired as best as 1893 technology would allow, Silas took me back to the farm. On the ride back he told me that he had lost his wife two years ago after only five years of marriage . He told me all about her life and how she was one of the most devout Christians he had ever known. I told him that I was never much of a church goer, but since time-traveling, I was giving more thought to religion. When he invited me to go to church with him the next day, I immediately accepted. It was then that I got a huge surprise when Silas stepped up to the pulpit after putting on his collar. He was the town minister. Life was going to be quite interesting with this man, I thought, but I had no idea how long I would be with him or if I would ever return to my own time.

"Nearly two hundred people crammed into the small church, filling every seat and standing against the walls. Children sat in the center aisle and the small choir of eleven stood behind Silas. All the windows were open, allowing a nice, cool breeze to flow throughout the crowded space. The choir members sang beautifully, and Silas had the congregation in the palm of his hand when he preached. It was an awe-inspiring service and for the first time in many years, I felt the spirit of God flooding my body and soul. After the service, we assembled in the picnic grove for a light lunch and refreshments. Not wanting to create any kind of ruckus, Silas introduced me as his cousin, Ellen, from New York City. I was bombarded with questions about living in the city, which I had to wing, making up answers as I went along."

6

"Three months had passed by rather quickly. After my ankle and elbow healed, leaving me with a slight limp and an arm that would not completely straighten, I helped Silas plow the fields and plant the crops, letting the watering schedule up to God. In the afternoons I cooked the meals, which would mainly consist of raw or cooked vegetables, and the meat would be whatever Silas was able to trap or shoot. I had to learn to eat squirrel, deer, prairie dogs, and elk, along with wild turkeys. I had never been a big meat eater, but I needed the protein to keep my strength up. Being a farmer's wife in the 19th century was very tedious work. Oh, that was a slip of the tongue. I could never be Silas' wife because I was his cousin, but my sexual appetite had been stunted when I wound up in the past. About two months after I arrived, Silas and I made love for the first time and it became a part of our lives. I was falling in love with this strong, handsome, farmer-preacher. During the quiet evenings I would regale him with stories about the life I had in the 20th century and he would fill my heart with stories from the Bible.

"We continued living this way for the next fourteen years and then a surprise came into our lives."

7

"Working in the field at the exact spot where I had arrived all those years ago, picking up rocks and placing them into the wagon, I felt a chill, as though winter had just fallen upon me. The feeling was brief, but when I looked at the spot, I saw a little brown and white dog. I wondered where it had come from and I called it over to me.

"He wore a Dallas Cowboys collar, showing the name Riley. His tag read Riley, 1721 River Road, Hellertown, Pa., and the tag was issued in 2012. I stroked his fur and said, 'Hi, Riley. Welcome to 1907.' Riley jumped up on me and kissed my cheeks and my lips, and I vowed I would take care of him until his death, my death, or our return to our respective time periods.

"When Silas came into the house later and saw him, he said, 'Well what do we have here?' He knelt on the floor and Riley rushed over to him, sniffing, and then licking him all over the face.

"Excited to have a puppy, I said, 'His name is Riley and I found him in the field where I appeared. Silas, he comes from the year 2012!'

"It didn't seem to matter to him because he kept ruffling Riley's fur and accepting all his kisses. 'What breed of dog is he, Ellen?'

"Stoking Riley's back, I responded, 'In the future, there are a lot of mixed breeds. I think this one could be a combination of a Labrador Retriever and a Springer Spaniel. He sure is cute, isn't he?'

"'Very,' Silas replied, standing up. At least his appearance will be a little easier to explain than yours. Do you think his appearance might mean anything as far as time-travel is concerned? I must admit, I think your time must be wonderful in which to live, considering all the conveniences people of the twentieth century have at their disposal. As much as I love you, I do hope that you will be able to return to your home someday.'

"After dinner, Riley curled up on the floor next to the stove, Silas sat in his rocking chair and I sat at the kitchen table, knitting a sweater, having learned the craft at a church social. Although my heart was still in 1985, or, if time ran at the same pace when one went back to the past, 1999, I loved this man and it wouldn't take very long to fall in love with Riley."

8

"The day that I spoke of came five years later, almost in the same way as I arrived in 1893.

"The three of us had been curled up in bed, enjoying the warmth of a quilt I had only finished making three days before. When I opened my eyes, I was treated to one of the most magnificent sunrises I had ever seen as the inside of the house turned almost entirely red for a few moments. Silas was beginning to awaken, and Riley was still asleep between us. He had his back against me, and his head was facing the bottom of the bed. I always hated when he was in that position because he would sometimes fart during the night and there was nothing worse than the smell of a dog fart under covers.

"I enjoyed the moment for a long time and then Silas opened his eyes to witness the sight. 'Wow,' he uttered, and that sound was enough to awaken Riley. The dog, whom we thought to be perhaps six years old, abruptly stood up and worked himself from under the quilt. He stood in an attack position and barked at the color a couple of times before turning a full circle and lying down between us again.

"I turned to Silas and, in an emotional voice said, 'Honey, I have a terrible feeling that I am going to be leaving you today and going somewhere else in time.'

"He sat straight up. 'What gives you the feeling that today is the day?' he asked, as he wrapped his arms around me.

"I looked at him, my heart nearly breaking, and replied, 'I am not sure, but I think it might be a combination of factors that are leading me in that direction. Have you ever seen our house flooded with red sunlight like this before?' He shook his head and I heard him swallow an emotion. 'When I awakened, I felt a tingle, much like the one I felt just before I disappeared in 1985. The tingle wasn't as great, but I think it might be a warning that I'm going to be leaving shortly.' I kissed him and then Riley decided he wanted to kiss us both too, making us laugh. I saw sadness etched in Riley's eyes and I thought he knew I that I was going to leave. Silas and I ruffled the fur around his neck and his head, and he let out a sigh like we had never heard before.

"After breakfast, Silas, Riley, and I headed out to the field to continue with the plowing. We were busy creating the planting rows. It seemed that no matter how many times any specific area was worked, we had to lift rocks by hand into the wagon and it was tedious at best, but it had to be done year after year. Riley was having a great time chasing birds and his tail when it got in the way. We were also singing the hymns we knew, as Riley sometimes howled along. Life was so good at this moment and then it happened.

"Silas had just begun to plow the row he was working on when I screamed his name. 'Silas! I am going! I love you! Take care of you and Riley!' He had turned when he heard my voice and little by little I vanished until I found myself in the warehouse in 1930 and then, of course, here in the TTF."

9

Back in his office, Nelson was reading emails when he came across this one from Saundra.

Silas continued living on the farm and leading his church in worship every Sunday. He never became involved with another woman and he passed away in his bed on June 19th, 1923.

Riley had been ten-months old when he disappeared. His family had been at the market and when they came home that day in 2012, their wonderful dog was gone. They placed flyers all over town and took out an ad in the area's largest newspaper, but the dog was never heard from again. After arriving in 1907, he was the constant companion of Silas and Ellen. After Ellen returned to 2013, Riley whined and pined for her every day until he died in 1920 at the age of 14.

Roger McKay
September 9th, 2001 to July 7th, 2013

1

"I went from being a billionaire to a pauper in the time one can snap his fingers, and I did not like it one bit.

"My company, McKay Investments occupied two floors of the North Tower of The World Trade Center and two hours before I vanished, I had received a call that I was now worth one billion, four hundred and nine thousand dollars, after closing a deal that put a multi-billionaire in my firm. I was elated. I was ready to celebrate my thirty-eighth birthday the next weekend and now I found myself in Wheeling West Virginia in 1931. I was wearing a three-thousand-dollar suit, along with a four-hundred-dollar shirt, a one-hundred and twenty-five-dollar tie, and a six-hundred-dollar pair of shoes. I arrived inside a coal mine that was pitch black and the dirtiest place I had ever been in my life. I did not grow up with a silver spoon in my mouth, but my family did okay money wise. At the office, eighty years in the future, my wallet and my car keys were inside the top left-hand drawer of my desk. I did not like to have them on my person when I was at work.

"A few moments later, I saw a light bouncing up and down and I called out, 'Hello?'

"The bouncing light stopped and then I had a powerful flashlight shining into my face. A voice said, 'Who are you and what are you doing in this section of the mine? It's dangerous here.'

"I identified myself. 'My name is Roger McKay and I must have time-traveled here. Less than a minute ago I was in my office in the World Trade Center and now I am here. Where the hell am I?'

"Two men, miners, I assumed, finally were standing by my side, staring at my clothing. 'Time-travel, you say?' One of the men inquired as they both laughed. 'So where is this World Trade Center you mentioned and what year did you travel from?'

"The sarcasm was thick, but I simply answered, 'The World Trade Center is in New York City and the year I came from is 2001. Now, will you tell me where and when I am?'

"'You are in the Cardley Coal Company mine number three in Cardley, West Virginia, and the year is 1931. Sadly, I have bad news for you, Mr. McKay. We are trapped in this mine and to be perfectly honest, my friend, I don't think we are going to get out of here alive!'

2

"I sat down hard, trying to digest the fact that I had somehow time-traveled to this place and now I was going to probably die, eighty years before I would be born. 'How much time do you figure we have?" I inquired through shaky lips.

Wiping off black water that was dripping on his face, he answered, 'Well, I'm guessing the oxygen will probably run out in three or four hours, and we haven't been in here long enough to warrant a rescue effort. The mine is closed today, but we were sent in to check on the supports in this section. Yesterday several workers said they heard timbers cracking, but the company is so damn cheap that they won't pay for repairs until they have actual proof that the timbers need shoring up. Sadly, they do, so it's possible that they might even fail before the oxygen runs out and we could be crushed to death.'

I laughed, sardonically and said, 'You guys sure know how to make a guy feel good, don't you? Do you have names I can call you?'

"'Mister McKay, sometimes in the face of grave danger, one must maintain a sense of humor to keep from going insane. Maybe, with your extra hands, we can at least repair the supports to give us a little extra time. So, what do you say we get to work? Oh, I'm Elias Saunders and this strapping young man is my son, Jake.' His eyes grew sad.

"I replied, 'But if we begin work, won't we be using up more oxygen, giving us less time? I'm not a miner, but what we're discussing isn't rocket science.'

"Jake responded, 'Well, you do have a point. Besides, we sure don't want to work ourselves to death, now do we?' He laughed maniacally.' As his father shook his head.

"We sat down to conserve our energy and the miners wanted to know everything about the future; a future they certainly could have only dreamed about.

"I talked for about an hour, my throat was parched as hell, but there was really nothing else to do. Elias offered me a sip from his canteen, even though there was only a little tepid water left inside.

"When I figured that I had told them everything I could remember, we relaxed. The air was becoming staler and to make things even worse, their miner's helmets lights and the flashlight were beginning to fail as well, until we were in complete blackness.

"I fell asleep.

3

"When I awakened, I had traveled to the warehouse in 1930, where many other travelers had gathered.

"I spoke to several of the time-travelers, listening to their adventures with great interest and after those conversations, I thought about all the things I had in 2001 and left behind, but more so, I thought about those two miners and how hard they had to work to provide for their families and then they died before even reaching the age of forty. I was an incredibly lucky man and I vowed that if I would ever get back home to my time, I would become the most generous man on the planet.

4

Two days after Roger McKay bounced back to 1930, an airplane hit the North Tower of the World Trade Center one floor above the two floors his company owned. Every employee was killed, and it would take years to divide up McKay's fortune, since he had no will at that time. He had been declared dead; his body never having been found.

Heather Newman
November 24th , 1999 to July 7th, 2013

1

"I was so looking forward to the upcoming four-day Thanksgiving weekend. I remember I raced home from school and dropped my books on my desk. My mom had laid my new dress on the bed and I wanted to try it on. I shucked my jeans, leaving my Freedom Football T-shirt on and pulled the dress down over my head. When I looked at myself in the full-length mirror on my closet door, I was very happy with the dress. Of course, my Nike sneakers looked weird with it, but I had a great pair of high heels that would sure look good on my dainty feet.

"The annual Turkey Day game was scheduled for ten o'clock and the stands were going to be filled with fans from both teams, a rivalry that had been going on for many years. My boyfriend was a receiver and he was having an awesome season. Tomorrow night we were planning to see the new movie, *End Of Days* . I'd been a supernatural horror buff since I was a kid and loved how authors and movie makers created these stories. I had hoped that someday I would be able to write a great horror or supernatural novel.

"I took off the dress and pulled on my Freedom Patriots sweatshirt and sweatpants, ready to head out the door for a quick run before dinner. My homework assignments were light, and I figured I'd finish it before *Buffy* and *Angel* came on TV. I loved those shows.

"I decided to run to the school and do a couple of laps around the track, but just before I arrived, I was grabbed by a man in dark clothing and he pulled me into an alley. I was certain that somebody saw my abduction because I heard some yelling from not too far away. He was strong as an ox and I couldn't break free from him. Once we were in the alley, he punched me in the stomach, doubling me over and knocking the breath from me. When I recovered, I felt what seemed like a jolt of electricity coursing through my body and I blacked out.

2

"When I regained consciousness, I groaned out loud, opened my eyes and stared into the mouth of an exceptionally large horse, whose rider was laughing hard.

"I screamed, 'What the hell is so funny, Mister? And your horse needs his teeth brushed.' I stood up and saw that I was in the middle of a muddy dirt street on what looked like the set of a western movie. I was truly perplexed.

"'Well, young lady, you caught my horse by surprise laying in the street like that.' He hopped off his mount and added, 'And where in the *hell* did *you* come from?' Hell came out a little more loudly than his other words.

"I studied him. He was about six feet tall, perhaps a hundred and eighty pounds with the brightest hazel eyes and a large smile. His teeth were a little yellow, though, and then she saw the small cigar between his fingers. He was dressed like a cowboy from the 19th century and he wore a pistol in a holster on his right leg. 'I can't explain how I got here, but I was running toward the football field in Bethlehem, Pennsylvania, when I was abducted by a man dressed all in black wearing a hoodie. My name is Heather Newman, I am sixteen years old and I am a junior at Freedom High School. I am going to graduate next year, which is the year 2000.'

"His jaw dropped, and he was speechless. When he was able to reply, his voice was not more than a whisper, as people were walking toward us. 'I don't think you should say anything more, Miss Newman, because some of these townsfolk would probably lock you up. You are in Braddock, Kansas, and the year is 1888. I'm Christopher Lollar, the town blacksmith.'

"Before too long, as we stood there, with about a dozen 'townsfolk' staring at me, a man broke through the assemblage and approached me. 'Hello, Miss. I am Jack Tanner the sheriff and I think we need to have a talk. You just appeared here from nowhere and I do not want these fine people to panic. I am going to ask you some questions and then we will see what we are going to do with you. I'm going to send my deputy to my house and have my wife bring some suitable clothing for you to change into.' As he took my arm and escorted me to the sheriff's office, gunfire rang out down the street. I turned and saw it was a couple of guys firing into the air. I was certain they had just come out from the saloon. Many times, I had wondered what it would be like to have lived in the Old West, and now I was going to find out firsthand.

3

"The sheriff offered me a seat and a guy inside the lone cell whistled at me. 'Ben Carson, you stop that,' Sheriff Tanner yelled, 'This nice young lady is not like the floozies you travel with. Give her some respect.'

"I couldn't help but laugh, and Sheriff Tanner smiled. 'Sheriff, where I come from, guys whistle at girls all the time. Usually I just flip them off, and then they just keep moving on.'

"Cocking his head, he asked, 'What do you mean, flip them off? I'm not familiar with that term.'

"'We stick our middle finger up in the air. It means fuck you.'

"Taken aback with my language, Sheriff Tanner said, 'You will please refrain from cursing around me. I am a Christian and I will have no part of it.'

"I apologized and promised I wouldn't do it again. *At least in his presence*, I thought. 'So, what would you like to know, Sheriff?' I asked.

"In a softer tone, he inquired, 'First of all, Miss Newman, I'd like to know where you are from and how did you just appear in the middle of the street?'

"Again, explaining what happened, I told the sheriff the same thing I told Christopher. 'How I managed to travel through time is certainly above my pay grade and I can't even begin to explain it.'

"Puzzled, Tanner asked, 'What does that mean, 'above my pay grade'?'

"I chuckled. 'It means that I don't have the knowledge to answer that question. Someone much smarter than me would be the one to ask, but I don't think we'll find that person in 1888, Sheriff. Could I have some water please? I'm really thirsty?'

"Tanner poured some cloudy water into a less than clean cup, but I drank it in a hurry, not even concerned with the number of bacteria I may have just swallowed. There was no other choice and I figured that as long as I was here, I would have to do as everyone else did. I thought I might be able to teach them some hygiene during my stay. Which reminded me that I had no place to stay and no money to rent a room. There was an empty cell next to Ben Carson, but I didn't think spending the night with him that close would be my best option.

" The sheriff capitulated. 'Obviously, if you *are* from the future, you have no family here, so I'm going to have to figure out where you can stay and what you can do to earn your keep.'

"Ben shouted out, 'She's such a purty girl, Sheriff, I bet she could make a lot of money dancing at Miss Belle's saloon.' He cackled and fell on his cot.

"Tanner yelled, 'Ben Carson, you stop that kind of talk. Miss Heather is only sixteen years old. I'll not send her to Miss Belle.'

"I stood up and stated, 'Sheriff, I do not think that is such a bad idea. Actually. I think I am *purty*, too, and I could show all the customers some moves on a stage. I certainly will not take my clothes off while performing, but since I do not want to wash dishes or any other mundane job, I would like to give it a shot. How about it? Please take me to see Miss Belle.'

4

"Fifteen minutes later, after telling Belle Wilk all about myself, she said, 'Heather, I think I would like to give you a chance. My girls do not sell their bodies because they make plenty of money dancing, and you are certainly attractive enough to keep customers in the saloon. I will give you a shot, as you like to say. All my girls stay in rooms above the saloon, and I will set you up with Marie Nolan. She is the closest to your age at eighteen. You won't have to worry about any clothing because we have many costumes you can choose from in the dressing rooms. I'll give you a dollar a day, plus your board, and you keep whatever money the gentlemen throw up on the stage. You can start day after tomorrow.'

"Feeling gratuitous, I smiled. 'Thanks, Miss Wilk. I appreciate the opportunity to make a few dollars.'

"She nodded. 'Please call me Belle. You will be in room 24, up the stairs and two doors to the right. Marie will probably be resting so knock lightly before you enter.'

"I knocked three times and heard her say, 'Come in.'

"She smiled and offered me a seat on a comfortable cloth chair after I introduced myself.

"When she began asking me questions about my life and my family, I had momentarily thought about lying my way through our conversation, but I decided to cut to the chase and tell her the truth.

"When I finished, she stammered, 'You are still in school at sixteen? I had to leave school when I was twelve to help Ma and Pa around the farm. We were too poor to hire any hands, so's my brother Edwin and I had to do many of the chores that grown men would normally do. It was hard work and after three years I couldn't take it anymore. I run off and wound up here in Braddock where I worked as a waitress and when I was seventeen, I started dancing for Belle. She is a really kind woman, and she won't let any of the men who come to see us treat you badly.'

"Marie and I talked for a long time and then she showed me around town, which wasn't much. There was a three-story hotel with a restaurant on the first floor. The businesses included a mercantile, a feed and seed store, the jail, a livery for the horses, a small school, and a church, along with Belle's place. The buildings were extremely rustic and not well kept. I saw several single homes along the main street, and they were maintained nicely with flower beds in the yard and grass was growing on the lawns. I thought the wealthier people lived in these houses and Marie told me I was correct. After our tour, I became very tired and decided to take a nap.

"A couple of hours later, I heard music from downstairs, so I headed down to watch the girls perform to a piano player, a guitarist, a snare drummer, and a trumpeter. I thought the music was much livelier than I would have guessed. I was supposed to start working in two days and as I watched the others, I came up with a few ways to use my 20th century athletic abilities. I would need some props and I asked Belle if she could get these items for me.

5

"On August 18th, 1888, my seventeenth birthday in 2003, I stood in the wings waiting for Marie to finish her act. The building was filled to capacity because word had gone to nearby towns that a new girl would be performing at Belle's Saloon. I was kind of feeling like a rock star, even though the stunts I was going to perform could be done by any cheerleader or gymnast in the future. It was going to be fun. I was even going to borrow a famous scene from one of my favorite movies.

"A couple of days ago before opening, and with only Belle present, I explained what I was going to do for my final dance of the evening. I had taken the time to set up the props and I did a run through for her without music. I told her what kind of clothing I wanted to wear, and she told me she could make them for me. 'Heather, honey, when your act is over, every man out in the audience will love it so much that I feel someday you will be on a much bigger stage than mine, performing for larger audiences too. I will get everything ready for you in time for your performance.'

"When I took the stage, I began with a couple of flips. My costume would have hardly even garnered a second glance in 2003, but in a black one piece outfit that looked much like a modern day bathing suit, along with black cloth wrapped around my calves like warmup leggings, I was showing off more skin than many of the men watching had probably ever seen outside of their bedrooms or in a whorehouse.

"I pranced and slithered across the stage like a snake, shaking my bottom at the men at every opportunity. When two long, narrow cloths dropped from the ceiling, I began to climb them, wrapping them around my feet, hanging upside down and after a few minutes of this, I slid back down to the stage for my finale.

"I raced off stage and grabbed a wooden chair, placing it in the center of the stage, looking up to make sure I had it at the correct place. After busting a couple of moves, I sat in the chair and then stretched myself out, pulling a cord that emptied a bucket of water all over me, splashing the first couple of rows of spectators. I bowed and then did a split dropping my face to the stage floor. My *Flashdance* moment awarded me with a five-minute round of applause and twenty-five dollars was thrown on the stage for me."

6

"During my stay in the 19th century, I had opportunities to go to New York City to work in the finest Burlesque houses and I would have been able to earn a great deal of money, but there was always one thing holding me back from that great adventure; Christopher Lollar. I had fallen in love with the young blacksmith after living in 1888 for all those months. He was an intelligent conversationalist and then there was the night when I became a woman. Although only seventeen, I was physically and mentally ready for sex and Christopher was gentle and kind, going slow when I needed him to and fast when I was ready. He told me that he had only been with two women in his young life, and he taught me well.

"I had been in the past for a little over a year when I found out I was pregnant. I knew I would have to give up my dancing job, and that was okay because I had managed to save quite a bit of money. When I gave Christopher the news, he was elated, and we immediately planned to marry very soon. His folks only lived about four hours away by stagecoach, and he wanted them at our wedding. Obviously, I had no family, except for Belle and the girls, but I decided we would have a huge reception in the saloon.

"Our town was growing and there was now a need for a second teacher. Sheriff Tanner recommended me for the position and I gladly accepted. I was really enjoying my life in the 19th century, but I also missed my time too.

"Christopher's business was growing, and he had to hire a blacksmith to assist him. Our wedding was a marvelous event and when Justin was born, I exploded with joy. I had a lot to learn about being a mom, but Christopher's mother came to stay with us for a couple of weeks to help me out. I had taken a six week leave of absence from my teaching job and when I returned to work, I became the best teacher I could be.

"Our lives were about as good as lives could be back then until a couple of days before Christmas in 1899. Christopher's parents were coming to visit for the holidays, but the stagecoach's front axle broke and the stagecoach rolled over several times, killing them both. Christopher was devastated and so was Justin. He was nine years old and he had spent weeks painting a picture for them for Christmas. By New Year's Eve, our lives were back to normal although we grieved every day for the loss we had suffered.

"Two days later, as I was preparing dinner while Christopher was working on the fire in the fireplace and

Justin was studying at the table, I felt a tingling sensation throughout my body. I knew I was leaving my husband and my son, and I just had enough time to tell them goodbye. They both knew this day could come, but as I disappeared, I saw the sadness etched in their faces.

"Moments later, I was in the warehouse in 1930 with all the other travelers and the TTIs."

7

Later that day in 2013, Nelson was reading the report about Christopher Lollar.

He continued to build his blacksmith business as the town grew larger. By the time he was thirty-seven, he had enough money to purchase the general store and three years later, he had added the livery and the Braddock Hotel to his empire. Sadly, he passed away at the age of forty-nine, but Justin inherited all of his properties.

Justin Lollar enrolled in college at Pittsburg State University in 1908 to study business and over the course of his four years of study he also played football. After graduating in 1912, Justin returned to Braddock and opened the first accounting firm in the town. Over the course of the next thirty-four years, he opened firms all across Kansas and Missouri, amassing a fortune along the way. His career was interrupted for a year and a half when he joined the army to fight in World War One. Justin was a combat infantryman and during his service, he was awarded two Purple Hearts, a Bronze Star, and a Silver Star. In the action that earned him America's third highest award for valor, Justin single-handedly destroyed a German machine gun nest that had his squad of five men pinned down for seven hours. One of the men he saved was Private Norman Younes, great-grandfather of Ken Younes, Time Travel Inspector.

Cletus Lassiter
January 1st, 1987 to July 7th, 2013

1

After reading the information found about Christopher and Justin Lollar, especially the revelation that Justin saved the life of Ken Younes' grandfather in World War One, Nelson took a little nap and then went to see the next traveler, Cletus Lassiter.

"I was nursing a monstrous hangover from the previous night's New Year's Eve party, celebrating my victory in the annual End of The Year Tournament at Veteran's Golf Club just outside of Sarasota, Florida.

"Having bounced back from three down with four holes to play. I birdied fifteen, chipped in for eagle on the drivable par four sixteenth and then on seventeen, I drained a twenty-five-foot downhill double breaker to tie the match. Eighteen was a tough par five of five-hundred and nineteen yards with water all down the left side. I had seventy-one yards for my third shot and nailed a sand wedge to sixteen feet to the right of the hole, leaving me a right to left putt. Craig Johnson, my opponent, and last year's champion was bunkered in two, but he blasted out to nine feet, downhill and fast. I studied my putt from all four sides and when I was ready, I struck the ball firmly to take out the break. The ball caught the right side of the cup and did a three-sixty before dropping in. Craig also studied his shot from every angle. He tapped the ball and it picked up speed as it headed straight for the hole, but at the last second, it broke away, and it lipped out. I tossed my putter in the air and jumped high, savoring my victory.

"I had gone to sleep around 3 AM, an hour or so after my wife had turned in. I watched her sleep for a couple of minutes before I crawled in beside her, wrapping my arms around her and giving her a peck on the cheek. When I awakened, I was alone. Startled, I sat up on the bed and found that I was in a hotel room. I stepped on the floor and hurried to the bathroom needing to pass the large amount of beer that had been filling my bladder. After finishing, I went to wash my hands and noticed the old-style sink and fixtures. When I went back out to the bedroom, I noticed the tiny TV perched on top of the dresser. I couldn't find the remote control, so I turned it on manually. It probably took a minute or so to warm up and when it did, the news show was in black and white. I sat down on the bed watching the newscaster as he reported about the president signing a new bill. The next thing I saw was Dwight Eisenhower sitting at his desk in the White House and he was speaking about Alaska becoming a state. I was floored watching news that had happened almost thirty years ago.

"Figuring it must be some kind of retro TV news program, I turned the dial until I found a show. It was *The Honeymooners*. Turning the dial again, I finally found another station that was showing a commercial. My eyes almost popped out as I watched Perry White, Jimmy Olson and Clark Kent selling Sugar Smacks. That commercial was followed by the Peanuts gang talking about the new Ford Falcon. Mesmerized, I waited for the next program to come on and it was *One Step Beyond*, which, at that moment seemed fitting. Somehow, I had gone to sleep in 1987 and awakened in 1959.

"Dressed in only boxers, I had no clue how I would be able to leave this room and find out where I was. Hearing water running in the adjoining room, I opened the unlocked door and tiptoed to the closet where some clothes were hanging. The pants and shirt were only one size larger, so I hurriedly dressed. On top of the dresser was a wallet. I opened it and took out all the cash, stuffing it into my pocket. I opened the dresser drawer and found socks, and there were several pairs of shoes on the floor. I smiled when I realized they were my size. I hated taking the guy's money, but I had no idea how long I would be in 1959, so I had to get off to a good start, moneywise that is. I opened the door and stepped out into the hall, then down the stairs to the lobby and out the door into the street."

2

When the hotel was no longer in sight, I stopped on the street and took the bills from my pocket. The guy had three hundred and eighty-seven dollars in his pocket. I figured I could keep myself fed and watered for at least a week and stay in a halfway decent place. If I chose a place that served breakfast with a room, I would even be flusher.

Thinking of breakfast was making me hungry and soon I spotted a restaurant. I stepped inside and sat down at a table. On the way in, I noticed a loose newspaper, so I grabbed it to see where I was and what was going on. The date was May 19th and I was in the town of Branville, Ohio. As I paged through the paper, an advertisement caught my eye. The Branville Golf Club was looking for a full-time employee to mow grass, rake bunkers, and other golf related jobs. I didn't know how I was going to get a job with no ID, but I hoped I'd figure something out before I would arrive there later in the morning.

I had to walk about a mile to get to the course and as I reached the crest of a hill, one of the most spectacular golf courses I had ever seen stretched out before me. Even at this distance I could see how well maintained the fairways and greens were. Many of the fairways were lined with stunning trees and the sand in the bunkers was the whitest imaginable. I really wanted to work here because most courses I knew of allowed employees free golf. I had to smile because playing golf with 1959 equipment would certainly be a challenge. I walked on, filling my lungs with fresh air.

3

"The clubhouse was quite opulent, and the pictures hanging on the walls in the lobby told me that the place had been built in 1923. Three and a half decades later, many renovations had taken place to bring the electrical needs up to code, and all the rooms had been upgraded. Most of this information was in a brochure I picked off a French Provincial table near the entry. I had to wait several minutes until the dining room opened. The aroma of coffee brewing had been wafting throughout the structure for about five minutes.

"I was working on my third cup of coffee of the day when a threesome sat down next to me at the counter. One man nodded to me and asked if I had a tee time. 'No, I don't. I only arrived in town last night and my clubs have not caught up with me. I walked here from my hotel and, I must admit, I don't think I have ever seen a more beautiful course. Hopefully, I will be playing in a couple of days. My name is Cletus, but I go by Clete.'

"The man took my hand in his and replied, 'Nice to meet you, Clete. I'm Lester Ulman and I know the owner. I can get you fixed up with clubs, balls, and shoes. Let's take a walk to his office and we'll get you geared up in no time.'

"We walked down a hallway on thick, plush carpeting, the walls adorned with pictures of professional golfers, and what Clete assumed were probably club champions of past years. He was impressed with signed photos of Palmer, Snead, Hogan, and Nelson-four of the greats of the time. Although Jack Nicklaus had not yet begun his career - he would become the national amateur champion this year - he had played the course two years ago and set the course record of sixty-one, playing from the tips. His scorecard was framed and hanging on the wall, alongside his picture.

"Lester knocked, heard a gruff, 'Come in.' and then he entered the office. The owner of the club, Mike Barnaby, stood when he saw his friend and me enter. 'Les, you S.O.B., how the hell are you? How was winter in Florida?'

"Lester shook his hand. 'It was great, Mike. This is Clete. He was sitting in the restaurant all by his lonesome and I need to get clubs, shoes, and balls, so he can play with us.

"Mike nodded, but he frowned. 'Our new rentals haven't arrived yet, but I can let him use my clubs, since he's going out with you.'

"My three new friends and I hit practice balls for about a half an hour before teeing off, and, although I could not hit the ball as far as I could in 1987, the ancient clubs felt pretty good and I was able to move the ball in any direction I chose. After hitting about twenty putts from various distances on the practice green, I felt I was ready. The bets were set up and I knew I couldn't lose more than fifty dollars, but knowing I could win several times that amount, I was mentally ready for our friendly match.

"We were playing skins-two tie, all tie-and it wasn't until the sixth hole, a par three of one hundred and nine yards, downhill, that a skin was won. On this first par three of the match, it was agreed upon that if a birdie would win

111

the hole, the total skins available would be doubled. Laughing, I added, 'What about an ace?'

"Lester shot me a caustic look. 'In thirty years, there have only been four aces on this hole, so I think we can have a side bet of a hundred dollars per man for a hole-in-one.' The other guys nodded in agreement, and when I hit the ball, with a slight right to left draw, the ball hit on the green and after two hops, spun back into the cup.

"I wound up playing one of my best rounds of golf ever, shooting a seven under par 64. While we sat in the bar after the match, having a few cold ones, Michael joined us and offered me a job as an assistant to the pro. I had told him I was looking for a job at the course in order to get free golf, and he felt that because I played so well, never having seen the course before, I would do better as an assistant than as a grounds crew employee. I was completely blown aw..."

Clete clutched at his chest as his face grew white and, when he tried to stand up, he fell on the floor. Nelson punched a number on his phone as he was dropping to his knees to attempt to resuscitate Clete before the arrival of the medical team less than a minute later, but he was certain the man was dead. In all these years, nobody had ever died in the facility, and although there was a standard operating procedure for a death event, Nelson had not read it in years. He would have to re-familiarize himself with what he was expected to do.

July 9th , 2013
One

1

With the exceptions of Dan Rodin and Clarissa Fortuna, all time-travelers and Time Travel Inspectors had been accounted for. Over the past four days, numerous interviews had been conducted with the returnees and they had been allowed to mingle with one another since yesterday morning. Doctor Nelson Wainwright was exhausted, and the staff had been given orders not to disturb him for anything. He had not had enough sleep since Dan had traveled backward in time to Gettysburg in 1863. His whereabouts were still unknown since July 7th when all the others had returned to the Time Travel Facility.

At 8:30 AM, Wainwright opened his eyes and sat up in bed responding to the sound of alarms and the ringing of his phone. He grabbed it from his nightstand and said, "Wainwright!"

"Doctor, please come to the transfer area immediately. General Rodin has just returned."

2

After disappearing from the bar on September 11th, 2001, Dan found himself in Danville, Virginia on August 18th, 2015. When he saw this date on a newspaper header, he was greatly confused because Nelson was insistent that travel to the future was probably impossible since future time still had not occurred. Apparently the most knowledgeable time- travel researchers had no idea themselves.

The large, freestanding clock in the town square showed the time was 5:47 AM and the town was still pretty much asleep. Dan saw a street sweeping vehicle lumbering along followed by a parking transportation vehicle. When he watched the street-sweeper go around a parked car, the transportation cop pulled up and moments later a young woman in uniform placed a citation under the windshield wiper of the car.

Dan strolled down the sidewalk peering into shop windows. He passed by a sporting goods store, a dress shop, a Rita's, and a bookstore. He had to smile when he saw a copy of *My Seventy-Five Years As A Time Traveler,* displayed in the window. He then saw a framed, signed photograph of Clarissa Fortuna, draped in black crepe paper. In front of the book and the picture was an obituary from three days ago revealing that the author had passed away on August 14th, at the chronological age of 94, although she had been alive for almost one-hundred and eleven years. Very few people would understand that, and he had difficulty with it himself at times.

A middle-aged man strolled over to Dan as he watched him stare at the display. "She was quite a lady. I read her book after it came out fifteen years ago and although the stories were hard to believe, I accepted them as her truth about time-travel. I'm Harvey Nesbitt and I own the restaurant a couple of doors up. I'm heading there to open. Could you use a cup of coffee?"

"Sure. Thanks."

"Are you new to town or just visiting?"

"Dan Rodin is my name and I'm just visiting. I only arrived here about an hour ago. My car is parked down the street a ways."

"Nice to meet you, Dan. Have a seat at the counter until I turn on the lights and get ready to open. I have the coffee maker on a timer, and it should be ready in a minute or two. My early birds will be here shortly and if they don't get their coffee within a couple of minutes of their arrival, they get a little edgy."

Moments later, four men and four women burst through the door, laughing their heads off. The look of pure joy was etched into their faces, and that alone brought a smile to Dan's face.

"Harvey, I hope that coffee is almost ready,' one of the men shouted. "Our tee times are in an hour, and we're anxious to get out there today. Oh, we also want bacon and eggs for all."

"I assume your wives are going to beat your asses again, aren't they, Ralph?"

As the eightsome sat down at a long table, Ralph replied, "Probably so, my friend, but who cares. Retirement is great."

When Harvey came back to the counter to pour Dan's coffee, the retired general said, "They sure are a happy bunch."

"Yeah, they are. All eight of them are retired military, and they all retired on the same day, two years ago."

"That's pretty interesting. Were they serving locally?"

"They were. The base they were stationed at was closing and all of them had been there for most of their careers, so they decided to pack it in instead of having to make moves at their ages. Of course, none of them are over fifty-five. All of them were officers ranking from two star down to light colonel. I looked up the retiree pay scale for those ranks, and they will be living high on the hog until they are old and gray."

"Why did the base close?"

"Budget cutbacks and the army decided to implode an underground facility that had only been there for about a quarter of a century. The facility was very hush hush, but the media had found out it was used for top secret research of some kind."

Beads of sweat rolled down Dan's face. "Where was the facility? I retired from the army about five years ago and I never heard of a place like that."

"The base and the hole in the mountain are about four miles north, but I don't think there is too much to see. Most of the buildings were demolished and you can't get close to the mountain because it's been fenced off, plus I heard there are sensors all over the place. I don't know why, but, obviously, you know the army. They tend to overdo things."

Dan laid a couple of bucks on the counter and said, "Thanks, Harvey. I've been a relic hunter all my life, so maybe if I poke around long enough, I can dig something up that had been missed. Do you recall the exact date the facility was imploded?"

"Yeah, I can. It was destroyed on July 15th, 2013."

3

While Dan hurried to the site of the old base, he was genuinely concerned that the Time Travel Facility was what had been destroyed. He wondered why, plus how he would get back to 2013 unless he would time-travel there prior to July 15th, six days from now in his real time. When he arrived, he saw that Harvey was right. There was little to be seen of the old base except for a few concrete structures. One could roam around freely, but the mountain was indeed protected by a high fence topped with barbed wire. Dan knew he had to get in there to explore, but he had no idea where the sensors were, if there were any at all, or if the area was monitored by cameras. When he looked toward the mountain, he saw that a piece of it had been blown to pieces and that new vegetation had begun to grow, covering the damage.

As he looked for a possible entrance, he also did a visual search for cameras or sensors, but nothing seemed out of place. He wondered if the area was under satellite surveillance, but he had no idea how to find that out. Dan walked around the entire fenced off area and found no way to get inside the perimeter. He decided to take a walk through the old base to see what he could find.

At the first concrete structure, he found three doors; all of them were padlocked. If he would have had a few tools, he probably would have been able to pick the locks, but again, he was thwarted. The windows were covered with large sheets of one-inch thick steel with bolts driven into the walls. No chance here, either, he thought.

He had begun to think that if there would have been cameras, soldiers would have arrived by now to apprehend him for trespassing.

Dan was circling the third building when he saw a small mirror laying on the ground. He picked it up and when he held it up to his face, he didn't see his reflection. A thought occurred to him that since he didn't exist in 2015, he wouldn't be able to see his reflection. That was a wild idea, but it was the only plausible one he could come up with.

When Dan smashed a lock on the door with a heavy stone, the man watching him through binoculars hopped in his car and headed to the building.

4

When Harvey Nesbitt pulled up beside the building, Dan was in the process of opening the door. He looked toward the car and saw the restaurateur sliding out from the vehicle. Nesbitt waved to Dan and strolled to the door. "I see you found the base okay. Not a whole lot here to look at is there?"

Dan took his hand in his and when Nesbitt pulled his hand away with a stunned look on his face, Dan shot him a quizzical look. "What's wrong, Harvey? I know my hand is a little rough after what I had recently gone through, but it can't be that bad."

"Dan, I couldn't feel your hand at all. When I grasped it, it was as though there was not a hand in mine." Harvey placed his hand on Dan's shoulder, and it went right through. He pulled back. "What the hell is going on here, General?"

"How did you know I was a general, Harvey? I sure didn't offer that information."

"Why don't we step into the building, away from prying eyes and then we can talk. I know for a fact there are no working cameras in the building, but there are many outside, even though I don't think I could find them with the way they are camouflaged."

They stepped through the doorway and were greeted with the smell of stale air. The door had obviously not been opened in over two years. Dan saw a handful of desks and chairs, and the walls were devoid of anything except for wires coming out through several outlets. The wires had been pulled out from electronic devices and they laid on the floor like so many coiled-up snakes. Dan walked to a desk and attempted to open the drawers, but they were locked, so he sat down in a leather office chair and turned toward Harvey. "So, what would you like to tell me, Mr. Nesbitt?"

Harvey took his iPhone from his pocket and focused the camera on Dan, taking several shots. No pictures of him came up on the screen and he nodded his head. He sat down in a chair, facing Dan, and said, "I am a retired Major General and I worked on this base for almost seven years before it was shut down. I never knew what kind of facility was in the mountain, and why it had to be imploded, but in late July of 2013, I was told to watch for you and kill you at the first opportunity. I had been in the army for thirty-five years and I had killed when necessary, but when my superiors would not give me any information about why you should be assassinated, I retired. What did you do that they want a general officer killed, Dan? I looked you up on Wikipedia and after reading your biography and seeing you disappeared on June 27th, 2013, I was hoping I would run into you someday to ask what the hell happened to you then and why are you a hologram now?

5

Back in 2013, before Dan returned, Nelson was in his office looking over the transcripts provided by the time-travelers and the TTIs. He couldn't concentrate on his job because Dan Rodin was always on his mind.

Looking at his watch, he saw he only had five minutes before his conversation with Ellis Westbrook, the final time traveler to be interviewed.

He answered one more email and then headed down to the interview room, knocking before entering. He saw Ellis sitting in a chair with a faraway look on his face, but a moment later, the look was replaced by a smile.

"I disappeared on March 23rd, 1991 and found myself at the bottom of a slate quarry filled with workers handling picks and shovels to break up large pieces of slate, loading them into huge containers that were attached to pulleys. As I watched the men work, one container was being pulled up and when it neared the top of the quarry, the cable snapped, and the container and contents were on their way back to the bottom of the quarry. Three men were crushed by the heavy load and several more were injured. Being a surgeon, I had no recourse but to help these men and hopefully keep them alive. The pieces of slate had cut them at numerous places, and I worked putting tourniquets on arms and legs and one guy had his guts spilling out when a piece of slate pierced his abdomen. I didn't know if I would have been able to save him, but I was certain that the men on whom I put the tourniquets would not lose their limbs. I had worked at a M.A.S.H. unit in Korea, so I knew how to perform triage.

"After all the wounded were tended to and the dead were taken out of the quarry in the containers, I sat down hard and lit up a cigarette. I was sixty-one years old and hadn't worked that intensely since my army career ended in 1979. The workers kept asking me where I had come from, but I had no idea how to answer them. They were so appreciative for me saving some of their buddies that they just stopped asking after a while. While I rested, I noticed a newspaper on a small table within reach. I pulled the paper from the table and scanned the front page. It was a copy of the Allentown Morning Call, although I didn't know how old the edition was. The date on the header was Wednesday, July 19th, 1916. Of course, I was shocked at my dilemma. How did I transcend time and find myself in a time and place seventy-five years earlier than where I had just been an hour earlier?

"As I pondered this question, a man came up to me and said, 'My name is Joseph Neirer, and I own this quarry, along with three others. After seeing how you treated those injured men, saving both life and limb, I would like to offer you a job as company doctor. I understand that I know nothing about you, but observing how you took care of those men, I am quite certain that you have had prior medical experience. If you already are employed, I will double whatever your employer is giving you and I can offer you a house in town. When you are ready to decide, please come up to my office and we will talk more.'

"He walked away without another word, but I certainly was going to take him up on his offer. I had no idea how much I should ask him for because salaries in this time period were obviously way less than in 1991. I opened the envelope and found that he had given me five hundred dollars. I decided to take a walk to the town of Slatington, Pennsylvania, about a mile down the road.

6

"I wound up at the Arlington Hotel where I had a meal and then got a room for the night to freshen up. After a nice hot bath, I got dressed and went outside, wanting to find some clothes appropriate for the time period and, after a short walk, I located a general store that had everything from soup to nuts. I selected nice slacks, a shirt, a sweater, shoes, socks, and underwear, asking the owner if I could change in his back room. I wanted to get rid of my anachronistic outfit.

"After dressing, I took my former clothes along with me, stuffing them into a large trash container beside the building, pushing the large brown paper bag as far down into the garbage as I could. I began walking around town. Passersby nodded to me and wished me a good day and I returned the greeting. I stopped by a garage and watched two men changing tires on old cars, while attendants were pumping gas, cleaning windshields, and checking oil in the vehicles that pulled in. I just found the old cars fascinating and the day passed quickly by.

"I was just about to enter the hotel when I felt my entire body tingle and I disappeared, winding up here. I hope Mr. Neirer wasn't too upset that I didn't come back after giving me all that money."

Nelson laughed loudly. "Joseph Neirer was not only the owner of several quarriers, he owned many homes and businesses in the Slatington area. He kept his small fortune through the depression, and when he died in 1951, he was worth twenty-four million dollars and change."

Ellis smiled. "I'm glad to hear that, Nelson. He was a really nice man."

The interview was over, and Nelson went back to his office.

July 9th, 2013
Two

1

Later, when Nelson entered the time-travel room, Dan was hugging his brother Harry. He could see the brothers were shedding tears of joy and he didn't want to disturb their moment.

After their reunion was completed, Dan saw Nelson standing a few feet away and he walked over to the director, offering him a hug as well. He whispered, "Nelson, I never thought I would see you again, and I know everyone in this room will want to spend a little time with me, and that is definitely okay. However, later, I want to speak with you, Harry, and Will somewhere we cannot be seen or heard, if there is such a place in this facility."

Not certain of what Dan meant, Nelson replied, also in a whisper, "To my knowledge, no one outside this facility can hear or see us," but he had second thoughts when Dan hugged him harder and said, "I have knowledge that we are being seen, but hopefully not heard, at this very moment. You must find a place we can talk. Our lives are in the balance." He quickly broke the hug and, smiling, he began to shake the hands of everyone in the transfer room.

Ten minutes later he was ushered into Doctor Blaine McCallister's office where he was given a complete physical, including an eye exam and blood work. When he exited the office nearly an hour later, Will Jennings was sitting in the hallway waiting for him. Will stood up and gave Dan a huge hug.

"Man, it is so good to see you again. You know they lost track of you and none of us had any idea where and when you went to, or how long you were gone."

"Good to see you too, Will. As to where and when I went, I have no idea. I just felt like I was in a void and I didn't know how long I was in there, but, according to real time, it was about a day. It felt a lot longer, though." He hated lying to his friend, but not knowing how much of the facility was being watched and listened to, he couldn't share where he had been until Nelson could provide a place where the outside influences could not listen in or see what they were talking about. He hoped there was such a place. If not, later today, he would have to tell everyone what was going to happen and reveal his plan to them. "Hey, Will, I'll catch you later. I really need some food and then I want to take a nap."

"Ok, man. See you later." He gave him another hug and then went back to his quarters.

2

Nelson paced around his office with many questions rattling around in his head, the main three being, *'"Dan told me that our lives are in the balance. Could that mean that my superiors are planning on destroying this facility and us along with it? If so, how will they explain our deaths to our families? How the hell did they bug this place without me knowing about it, and can I find out where all the bugs are placed and how to neutralize them? What is Dan planning, and how did he come to know all of this? Did he travel to the future?"*

He sat down behind his desk and pulled a copy of the Standard Operating Procedures from a locked drawer. He flipped through the book until he came to the Notes page, where he had penciled in several phone numbers. He punched in one number and texted a coded message. He prayed that the recipient would know what to do to answer the short message. In the meantime, all he could do was wait.

As he pretended to work, listlessly looking over reports and invoices of the new equipment that had been delivered yesterday, he wondered why they would be receiving new equipment if the facility was to be destroyed. He stood up and hurried to the warehouse to see what had been ordered and sent to the TTF.

He sought out Bill Ferry, the warehouse manager, and asked, "Do you know what the machines are that we just received and where they are going to be placed in the facility?"

"Doctor Wainwright, I have been trying to figure that out myself." He flipped through several sheets of paper on his clipboard until he found the specific information. He slipped the paper out from the stack and handed it to Nelson.

Nelson read it and was just as perplexed as Ferry, was. "This says that the machines should be placed at these eight specific spots and that instructions for their use would be emailed tomorrow." He took a photo of the paper and then handed it back to Bill. "I've never had any equipment come in before without first knowing about the delivery. I guess I'll have to make a call later to find out what this is all about. Thanks, Bill and have a great day."

"I will. Thanks. Do you want me to move the machines to their assigned areas?"

"I'll get back to you on that a little later. I want to check a few things out first." He walked away and headed to the IT department.

3

During lunch, Dan mulled over what he was going to do, knowing what he knew, and without extraneous eyes and ears seeing and hearing everything he would do and say. Cameras were located everywhere in the TTF, but were some of them monitored from the outside, and how could he figure that out. He considered several options but each one led back to the conclusion that his plans would be seen and heard by higher-ups outside the facility.

He finished eating and then strolled to his room where he laid down on the bed. He was totally exhausted. He felt that if he got at least a couple hours of sleep, he'd feel much better and could come up with a way to shut down those eyes and ears.

As he slept, he dreamt about his visit to 2015.

4

Dan updated Harvey about his time-traveling experiences since June 27th, 2013 and the retired major general listened intently to every word. When Dan was finished with his monologue, Harvey continued to stare at the black man totally mesmerized.

"Harvey, I think your superiors destroyed the Time Travel Facility to bury the fact that all those people traveled back to other times, and that there was no other way to keep the news from the world. They also killed my brother, my grandfather, and my friends. Somehow I have to get back to 2013 and stop this madness, but before that happens, if ever, I want to go to the TTF to see if I can find anything that can be used to expose what our government did and to get the truth out to the nation that time-travel did exist. Have you ever heard of any strange disappearances since the day the facility was imploded?"

"No, I haven't and I'm going to go with you to the site."

"No, Harvey, you aren't. I don't think they will be able to see or hear me because I am a hologram, but they would be able to see and hear you. I don't need you to die because of something that happened two years ago. You stay here and see what intel you can find on Google."

Dan walked out the door and ran to the mountain, hoping he'd be able to find something.

He arrived at a twelve-foot-high chain link fence with cameras on poles spaced every twenty feet apart. Electric Fence warning signs and No Trespassing signs were spaced out every ten feet as well. The fencing created a privacy screen disallowing viewing the mountain in the near distance. Since Dan was a hologram, he figured the cameras would not catch his image, but he was a little concerned about electricity running through the fence and he didn't know if a hologram could be electrocuted. He thought about climbing the mountain until he found a place where the fencing ended, but the fencing completely surrounded the area where the facility had been located.

As he pondered his options, he saw a rabbit squeeze under the fence, catching its fur with no electrical shock. He smiled; sometimes warning signs were enough. He reached out to touch the fence and his hand passed through the material. A moment later he followed his hand and was inside the perimeter with no harm done.

Dan strolled up the road until it ended at the base of the mountain. He had to assume this was the way he and Will were brought to the facility less than two weeks ago. The entrance was covered with rocks and vegetation, making access difficult even with heavy equipment, but he hoped it would be a piece of cake for him in his present condition. He stood in front of the rubble and placed both hands on the sea of rocks, sliding right through. The darkness was complete as soon as he passed through the debris and then he felt the heavy entrance door in front of him. He passed through very quickly and came upon even more rubble inside the imploded space. As he traveled forward, he occasionally came upon a small area that had not been affected and although it was dark as hell, he managed to find his way around by feel, finally coming upon a bank of desks. He opened drawers until he found a flashlight and an iPhone. There were also packages of flashlight batteries and an iPhone battery in the drawer.

He tried the flashlight, but the batteries were dead, so he replaced them. Holding an object in his hand was not difficult but turning the casing to open the flashlight was problematic and it took him long minutes to complete the task. He turned the flashlight, allowing the old batteries to fall to the floor and then he put fresh ones inside, He screwed the bulb back in and switched the light on, rewarded with a bright beam of light, which he shone around the small area to see what was there, hoping to gain a clue as to how the implosion was created. As he circled the space, he came upon a corridor that was partially destroyed and he decided to follow it to where it led.

5

In 2013, Nelson was fighting a splitting headache, so he entered his private bathroom and opened his medicine chest. He looked inside, seeing the meds he was taking to slow down his cancer, knowing he would never have to take them again, so he removed them and tossed them into his wastebasket. He found the extra strength pain meds and took four from the bottle, washing them down with a glass of tap water. He then stepped into his bedroom just to lie down a few minutes or so until the pills began to work. He managed to fall asleep for about thirty-five minutes and when he sat up, he felt much better.

He was wrestling with a plan for all the returnees. If he would release them, the knowledge of this facility would become public and enemies of the United States would want to take over the facility and use the technology and the wormhole to change the past to suit their evil goals. For those who had been gone for lengthy periods of time, their families would probably be in total shock when they saw them again. The case of William Wright, a husband and father, who disappeared from his cab in Los Angeles in 2000, and wound up in Bethlehem, Pennsylvania, in 1973, married a woman in 1982 and raising three kids, had caused Nelson great concern when he interviewed Wright four days ago, when Dan was in 1930.

As he continued to think over his options, his iPhone vibrated. The coded message was from Sylvia Warren, undeniably the most intelligent person in the facility She had checked her equipment and, by using a simple tool, a Geiger counter to which she had made some minor adjustments, she found that the facility was indeed being bugged, but she discovered two areas that the outsiders were not able to infiltrate. She also figured out a way to disable the cameras in these areas enabling anyone to talk there for an unlimited amount of time. She had not yet studied the new equipment, but that was next on her list.

6

After Dan walked through the entire facility, finding nothing of use, he worked his way back outside and hurried to the base, finding Harvey napping in a reclining chair.

He pushed a paperweight from the desk, and it crashed on the floor, awakening his new friend. Nesbitt rubbed his eyes and then saw the hologram of Dan Rodin standing in front of him. He smiled. "What did you find, Dan? Any evidence?"

Dan told him what he had found and then he said, "Harvey, there were no bodies anywhere. What the hell happened to the people?"

As Harvey listened to him, Rodin disappeared a moment before ten soldiers stormed into the room with their weapons trained on the retired major general. Moments later, three suits stepped into the room, forcing Nesbitt to sit while they read him the riot act.

7

In 2013, Dan entered the dining room and saw his brother, Harry, his friend Will Jennings, a woman he did not know, and Nelson Wainwright huddled at a booth near the wall farthest from the door. At this time of day, there were very few diners, and when he saw Nelson raise a cup, that signal prompted him to grab one from a rack and fill it with coffee. He then strolled over to the table and sat down, after he was introduced to Sylva Warren.

Nelson took a long look at the retired general before asking, "Dan, what happened to you and Clarissa when everyone returned through the portal two days ago? We tracked Clarissa and found her in Connecticut in 1997. After staying there, a short time, she traveled to and took up residence in New York City."

Dan smiled. "I'm glad you found her. It's a shame she didn't come here with all the other travelers and TTIs. But perhaps it was for the best..." His voice trailed off and he let out a sigh. "In six days, this facility is going to be destroyed and I have no idea what happened to everyone here."

He spoke for the next thirty minutes, telling them all that had happened to him since disappearing in 2001 and after relating his adventure in the TTF in 2015 he nearly broke down. "I could not understand why I didn't find any bodies in the areas that had not been completely imploded. Several barracks were unscathed and there was no evidence of violence. Bunks were made, inspection shoes and boots were lined up under the bunks, and the lockers were filled with freshly starched and pressed uniforms along with several civilian outfits for off duty time. It was as though everyone vanished. I think that is what bothered me the most about the near total destruction of the facility.

"I found several pockets with no damage including file cabinets, still filled with records and reports. A handful of computers had been untouched but when I tried them, there was no power. I checked out the electrical boxes and they were all dead." His hands shook as he lifted his coffee cup to his mouth. "Nelson, why will this facility be destroyed?"

8

At the base camp in 2015, Harvey Nesbitt was being questioned by the men wearing suits as soldiers kept their weapons trained on him.

"What are you doing here, General? You know this facility has been closed for two years and no one is supposed to enter any of these buildings!"

"Earlier, a man came into my restaurant and he was asking a lot of questions about this base. Of course, I played the dumb card and told him nothing. After he left, I followed him here but once he stepped behind this building, I never saw him again. I decided to come inside and check things out and then you guys showed up."

The men in suits relaxed somewhat and when they did, the soldiers lowered their weapons. One of the men said, "That is an interesting story, Harvey, but our cameras in your restaurant did not show any individual person talking with you, although we did see you in animated conversation with nobody. When I questioned the golfers, they claimed that they were the only customers at the time. So, who were you talking to, Mr. Nesbitt?" When he asked this question, the soldiers once again raised their weapons, training them on him.

Smiling, he replied, "Perhaps I was speaking to a ghost."

As he chuckled, he felt a huge fist smash into his jaw, knocking him off his chair and onto the floor. Nesbitt shook off the pain, opening and closing his mouth several times to see if his jaw was broken. Thankfully, it wasn't. He picked himself off the floor, righting his chair and sitting down in it once again, staring defiantly at the man who hit him. The man was shaking his fist and Harvey saw the pain etched in his face. "Gee, I hope you didn't break it, asshole," he barked, once again laughing through his pain.

The man reared back, ready to punch him again, but he was stopped by the obvious leader of the group, a man Harvey Nesbitt knew slightly from seeing him around town and serving him in the restaurant.

"Kennedy, what the hell is going on. I get being questioned, but your goon striking me is totally uncalled for. I've been watching for General Rodin, but he hasn't shown up."

"Calming down, Kennedy responded, "Okay, I believe you, but you must have some idea of who he was.

"The only thing I can come up with is that perhaps holograms have been created to mess with me in this ridiculous watch for Rodin. The man could be dead somewhere, maybe even in the TTF." As the acronym was leaving his lips, Harvey knew he had made a major mistake. He was not supposed to have known that the place was utilized for time-travel.

A scornful smile crossed Kennedy's face. "So, you do know what the facility was for. Now, I'm going to assume that Rodin came to you as a hologram to get information about its destruction. My friend, I think we're going to have a lengthy talk together today." Kennedy grabbed Harvey and lifted him from the chair to his feet. A moment later, the retired general reached into his pocket and pulled out a remote control. He pressed a button and within five seconds the entire building imploded, killing everyone inside.

9

In the dining room of the TTF, Nelson pondered Dan's question for a moment, with everyone staring at him, awaiting his answer.

"The only thing I can think of is that the powers outside this facility cannot allow anyone to leave, possessing the knowledge we have. They certainly can't send travelers to their homes after being gone for as long as many of them were. Blow the place up, kill all of us, and there will be nothing to answer for and nobody to answer to. If there is no evidence of the TTF having ever existed, there will be no questions asked. That's about the best I can come up with."

"Good enough answer for now, Nelson," Dan chimed in, "but how does that correlate with me finding no bodies?"

Nelson shrugged and shook his head.

"Dan, maybe you thought of a way to save us all and that's why there were no bodies found." Harry offered.

The general thought about this for a few moments and said, "That is possible, I guess. We still have half a dozen days left to figure this out, and I think we need to tell everyone what is going to occur, but where can we get them all together and let the cat out of the bag without prying eyes and ears watching and listening to us. I think we should just go about our business and meet here for coffee when necessary until we find a solution."

Without additional fanfare, the group stood up and went back to what they had been doing before gathering here. All of them were deep in thought as they left the dining room.

July 13th, 2013

1

Four days later, at three o'clock in the morning, the facility was quiet. Dan slipped out of bed and after a quick bathroom stop, he left his room, walking down the hallways toward the time-travel center. Since there were no travelers to monitor anymore, only a few people were working this shift. He nodded at a soldier sitting at a desk reading a book; his M-16 was lying across the desk in case he would need quick access to a weapon. He nodded at Dan and whipped off a salute to the retired general. Dan saluted back and nodded his appreciation. Except for the light being thrown out by the soldiers reading lamp, the subdued lighting along the walls offered just enough for Dan to traverse the paths without running into anything.

He arrived at the transfer room and opened the door. The green glow of the wall that was the portal to the past and back was darkened, but Dan could see that the borders of the entrance had the beginnings of a glow; it was always active he guessed. Dan walked right to the portal, his face less than an inch from the wormhole. He pushed his face forward and found it slid through to a different time period. He wanted to slide completely through to find out where he would end up, but he had a twinge of fear that he might not return to 2013 again. The knowledge that the facility would be destroyed in less than forty-eight hours propelled him through the wormhole. Dan would find out that he was now in Jamestown, Virginia, on March 14th, 1607. During his three hour long stay, Dan came to the realization that this trip to the past might be just what was needed to save everyone in the TTF.

He strolled back to the exact place he had passed through the mountain, after marking its location much like his brother and Will Jennings did when they left the facility to find him at Robert E. Lee's camp in 1863. Although the rock was solid, when he placed his hand on it, the wormhole opened, and he stepped back into the TTF to see Nelson Wainwright staring at him.

"Hi, Nelson, I guess you couldn't you sleep either?" As he spoke, he blinked SOS to the director.

"No, I've been having difficulty the past few days. I thought I heard noise in here and came to investigate, but now I have the hungries and I could use a cup of coffee. Care to join me?"

Sure, that sounds good. I don't think I'll have much luck getting back to sleep anyway.

2

At an army base less than twenty miles away from the TTF, Brigadier General Jefferson Davis, a distant relative of the Confederate president during the Civil War, was watching the action in the TTF. He saw and heard everything that was said until Rodin and Wainwright stepped out of view in the dining room. For some reason unknown to him, or any of the other flag officers monitoring the situation, they could not figure out why there were several dead zones in the facility.

Static was coming through his earbud and he didn't hear everything the two men said to one another and he desperately tried to read their lips from observing them through several camera angles, but the lighting was not the best and he was unable to filter in more light. He was concerned that the Rodin brothers, Will Jennings, and Nelson Wainwright knew that something was wrong and that they were being monitored. Davis had watched thousands of hours of video, seeing many of the travelers as they were on their inadvertent journeys and he had a twinge of jealousy, wishing he had been younger so he could have worked there as a TTI. When the facility opened in 2007, he was already over the age limit of thirty-five by fifteen years and a punctured eardrum, courtesy of an Iraqi bullet, ended his chances before he even had one.

Davis was one of the privileged few to know that the TTF would cease to exist in two days. He decided that after this assignment, he would retire. He was nearing sixty-two and he had been in the army for forty-three years. He understood that nobody could come out of the facility alive, but after this was over, he wouldn't be able to justify continuing to serve. He poured a cup of coffee and sat back as Rodin and Nelson walked into a dead zone.

He decided to scroll videos back several days, focusing on that specific spot in the dining room to see if there were other clandestine meetings. After several hours of viewing, he concluded that Wainwright knew something was going to happen soon, and he took the time to tell everyone working there, and every time-traveler his suppositions. Davis decided he had to inform his superiors about his conclusion that everyone in the facility was going to try to use the wormhole to go to the past where they couldn't be found. The facility would have to be destroyed by other means than the machines that were timed to explode on July 15th.

3

While Nelson quietly sipped his coffee and picked pieces from a chocolate covered doughnut, Dan told him about his adventure to 1607. When he concluded, he added, "I'm thinking that everyone should go through the portal, no matter where we wind up and begin our new lives there. At least we will live and deny the higher powers the opportunity to kill us all." His throat was dry after talking for nearly fifteen minutes straight and he guzzled down half a glass of water, wiping his mouth with his sleeve.

"Do you think we would wind up in Jamestown and become a group of settlers to the new country, or since you have returned from there safely, would we travel somewhere else? I'm also wondering if the portal would stay open long enough for almost a hundred people to go through and wind up at the same place."

"Nelson, your guess is as good as mine. If we would turn all the power back on, could we find out where we would be traveling to? Obviously, you could send TTIs back to where we had all traveled, but would that work if nobody is lost in time anymore?"

"Dan, that is quite an interesting thought. We never tried to send anyone back to the past just to see where they could be sent. Sadly, we have no time to experiment. I think you are right, though, we all must go somewhere, or we will all die. How will we get the word to everyone in the facility without being heard and seen? If we are attacked, we could hold our own for a bit, but would they initiate a ground attack, or just bomb this place back to the stone age? It would seem that it would take a hell of a lot of bombs. Have explosive devices been set in place when the facility was built? Do they have a way to render all of us unconscious and then come in to do their dirty work? Are the special machines going to explode-they were supposed to be set up at three specific locations? That scenario seems plausible since you said there were no bodies strewn about." He stared at Dan trying to read his mind and he wasn't afraid to admit that he was scared shitless.

Epilogue

1

At a dig on a blistering hot day in July of 2024, third year archeological student, Aiza Zafar, gently scooped dirt from a hole where a piece of pottery had been found. Having discovered the remnants of a previously unknown village, the project was now in its fifth year and more and more artifacts were being discovered every day. The foundations of nine buildings were revealed two years ago, along with tools and weapons carbon dated to the early sixteen hundreds. Although to date no graves had been discovered, the twelve team members concluded that the residents of the village most likely departed after living here for an undetermined amount of time. They had also found no evidence of any other villages within fifty miles during the remainder of the seventeenth century. The mystery of what happened to the people was first and foremost on the minds of the archaeological team.

The twenty-one-year-old American born Muslim, continued to dig a two-foot square hole and was down seventeen inches from the surface of the ground when her spade hit something solid-something metallic. As she removed soil from the top of the object, she scraped more dirt toward the sides of the hole and the rusty metal container was roughly a foot long by about a half a foot wide. As she continued to dig around it, she found the height to be about eight inches. Its construction was certainly not from the seventeenth century, but more like a twentieth century ammo box. She had seen many of them from the time she was a little girl and her father was a soldier.

During the time she had been digging around the box, she took numerous photos on her iPhone to record the discovery, and upon completion of this chore, she sauntered to the tent where equipment was set up and several team members were working on artifacts that had been found at the site by cleaning, labeling, wrapping, and finally placing them into storage containers.

The lead archeologist, Doctor Tran Li Yeager, a professor of American History, saw her step into the tent and shouted out, "Aiza, my favorite student, what brings you into my tent? Have you made a miraculous discovery that demands my attention, or could you have other amazing news?"

Yeager strolled toward Aiza and gave her a hug, thankful that all known viruses had disappeared from the face of the earth in 2022. "How are you?"

Beaming from ear to ear, Aiza told the professor about her discovery as they walked to where the box was still resting beneath the earth. Aiza wanted to open the ammo box, but she felt that Tran should have the opportunity to lift the box from its former prison and carry it back to the tent before it was opened. The container would have to be cleaned to see if there were any visible markings to determine who put it there and why. Obviously, it had been placed there sometime in the last eighty years. Aiza had Googled it on the way to the tent and found metal ammo boxes were first used during World War Two.

The two women arrived at the site, along with several team members who would take pictures and videos of the removal of the box. Getting down on their knees, Tran and Aiza reached in and lifted the ammo box from the hole. The insignificant weight of the container revealed that there was nothing heavy inside and their imaginations were running wild with ideas of the contents.

2

Mystified that such an anachronistic artifact would be found at a four-hundred-year-old dig, Tran pondered how or why the metal ammo box was placed at this particular place, but she assumed her question would be answered very shortly.

Kevin Langley, the metal expert of the team, grabbed a container of metal rescue gel from the back of his pickup truck. He also picked up a large paintbrush and several old towels, carrying them back to the tent and setting them on the table next to the ammo box. He wanted to see what kind of ammunition would have been carried in this box before opening it up. He was former military, having served with the 1st Infantry Division in Iraq, where he earned two Purple Hearts for his wounds, neither of them life threatening.

"Tran," he said, although speaking to everyone, "this process will take about twelve to twenty-four hours to complete as I have to apply the gel and then wrap the box to keep the application moist before I wipe it down tomorrow. The latch and handles are rusted fast to the box, and I fear if I would try to force them open, they might break, making the opening more difficult. I know we are all anxious to find out what is inside, but after dealing with booby traps, I want to be exceptionally careful before opening the container. I'll see how far along the rust bath has gone after breakfast."

"Okay, Kev, thanks. Well, people, we have several hours of daylight left, so I suggest we continue working to see if we can come up with anything else today." The twelve members of the team returned to their specific areas of the dig.

3

Returning to her area of the dig, Aiza decided to widen the hole where she found the ammo box, hoping to find more items that might have been buried along with the military container. Still not understanding why a twentieth century ammunition container would have been buried here, she went about her work at a faster pace than normal, expanding the width of the hole threefold, and finding nothing.

Moving to another small area, less than two feet away from where she had been digging, she dug down about eighteen inches and her spade hit something again. Her problem was that dusk was beginning to darken the woods as she wondered whether the contents would be uncovered before nightfall.

After dinner, she sat down on a bench near the campfire. She sipped on a glass of red wine as the team discussed the day's events. Aiza decided not to say anything about the second container she had found, her imagination running wild with what the contents could be.

Two glasses of wine later, her eyelids became extremely heavy and she decided to pack it in for the night. It was a few minutes after nine but working on a dig all day in this heat took a toll on a person's body. She wished everyone a good night and headed to the tent she shared with Tran, they being the only women on the team.

4

Aiza's eyes opened, when she inhaled the scents of bacon and eggs frying on a couple of grills outside. Her mouth watered and her belly grumbled. She unzipped her sleeping bag and sat up, looking toward Tran who was still softly snoring on top of her queen size air mattress.

She stood up and slid into a pair of shorts, a Titanic t-shirt, socks, and her work boots, and then nudged Tran awake. "Boss, bacon and eggs are on the grill, hustle your butt before the men eat everything." She laughed and sauntered out to the cooking area.

Grabbing a plate and utensils, she got in line behind two burly young college men, waiting her turn to be fed. After the students filled their plates, another man laid scrambled eggs on his spatula and gently placed them on her plate. Aiza requested three slices of crisp bacon, and one scoop of home fries. She moved away from the grill and strolled to a table where there were slices of toast, bagels, and English muffins, along with tubs of butter and jam. She grabbed half a bagel and a small amount of butter and jam. Finally, the young woman picked up a banana and poured a glass of orange juice before sitting down at a picnic table, devouring her meal in short order. She carried her plate, plastic glass, and utensils to the wash station, where she cleaned everything and placed them in the drying area. She hurried to a Porta-Potty and, after she finished, she washed her hands and applied sanitizer. She was so ready to see the ammo box opened and as she walked toward that workstation, she saw her co-workers begin to gather around the table, where Kevin Langley was waiting for the stragglers to show up, including Tran.

5

Kevin removed the towels that were saturated with gel and bits and clumps of rust. He grabbed a fresh towel and wiped the residue from the container. Grabbling the handle, he felt it give and he pulled it outward and upward until the lid disengaged from the walls of the container. He pulled out a garbage bag that was sealed with duct tape and he took his time removing the tape that was still quite pliable. He removed the bag to only find another, also sealed with duct tape. After repeating this process three times, he opened the final bag, pulling out a leather-bound journal. The leather was still remarkably soft, leading him to believe that it had not been buried for too long. Raised characters on the journal revealed that the owner of the volume was a man named Nelson Wainwright and it was dated 2013.

Telling that to the team sucked the oxygen from their breaths, as they were thinking the journal could have been from an earlier time period. Kevin opened the cover and began to read the quite legible tiny handwriting filling each line of the first page.

June 27th, 2013-Today I found that an old friend, Brigadier General Daniel Rodin was sent to the past via a mini storm that affected only a small area around where he had set up his tent for an overnight stay in the woods near Chambersburg, Pennsylvania. He was on one of his quests to find Civil War artifacts and wound up near a Confederate camp in 1863. Knowing he could be in real danger, being a black man, exclaiming to his captors that he was a general in the United States Army, I decided to send two Time Travel Inspectors back to offer him some protection during a time when blacks were not looked upon favorably. He was taken to meet the legendary General Robert E. Lee, who decided to treat Rodin as a prisoner of war. TTIs Ken Younes and Arlen Behr were selected to guard him while Lee rode to talk to his friend, General James Longstreet, whose army was camped several miles from Lee's headquarters.

Having the ability to see and hear what was going on in 1863, through the eyes, ears and mouths of Rodin, Younes and Behr, the team here at the Time Travel Facility was able to make quick decisions on how to handle the situation. That also applied to the inadvertent travelers, known to us as bouncers, who were trapped in different time periods of our history. Each bouncer had always at least one TTI nearby .

Kevin stopped reading and stared at his captive audience, seeing many different reactions, mainly curiosity. Just eleven years ago, time-travel had been perfected to the point where people from today could be sent back in time to keep watch over those who were not sent back though the Time Travel Facility. Digesting this was somewhat of a stretch for Kevin Langley who was a firm believer in science, not science fiction. *Would someone plant something like this as a scam?* He took a few moments to Google Nelson Wainwright and there was absolutely no information about that name in his search. He shared this with his team and then Aiza said, "I found another ammo box just before dark yesterday. Perhaps more light will be shed on this when we open it."

6

While Aiza and several team members went to her dig to retrieve the box, Kevin began flipping through pages, occasionally reading a story about a time traveler, marveling at the elaborate hoax that persons unknown perpetrated. After turning a few more pages, he discovered an envelope. Opening it, he found a list of names titled *Travelers, TTIs and TTF Employees now living in 1607. He* counted the names, arriving at a total of eighty-three, and one name caught his eye. It was someone his dad knew who disappeared from the face of the earth many years ago and had never been found. Kevin was beginning to form a different opinion of what he had thought a hoax.

Hearing voices nearby, Kevin looked up and saw the team members carrying another box, much larger than the ammo box, constructed of heavy-duty plastic. They arrived at his table and placed it in front of him. There was some rust on the metal parts of the latch, but with a little elbow grease he was able to loosen it quickly.

While he worked on the latch, he shared what he had found in the journal and asked for a volunteer to continue reading though the book and jotting down notes. That person was Peter Quinn, a thirty-two-year-old journalist, and a well-known speed reader. Perhaps after the entire book was digested and finding out what was buried in this container, the mystery might be solved. *Does time travel exist?*

He opened the latch and peered inside the box, gasping with eyes as wide as those of a child on Christmas morning.

7

Kevin began pulling out badges with readable names printed on them. He laid them out on the table, urging team members to grab a couple and look up the names on Google. He also found several thumb drives that he wanted to check out himself. He extracted many wallets, both men's and women's, assorted pieces of jewelry, iPhones and cellphones, small bottles of prescription medications, small bibles, a baseball signed by Babe Ruth encased in a plastic box, and a couple of journals. There was so much to study and catalog that Tran suspended all digging projects until further notice.

Several team members began to search the names on the IDs on Google, coming up empty. Driver's licenses were checked using state databases without success. By dinnertime, not one shred of evidence that these people had ever existed had been found.

Dinner was a simple affair of hot dogs and potato salad.

When everyone had filled their plates, they grabbed lawn chairs and placed them in a circle, giving everyone the opportunity to see and hear one another. Tran stood up and said, "Okay, let's go around the circle from my left and share what we found today with our specific areas of research, but I want to save Peter's comments until the end. He told me what he discovered, and you will all want to hear it." She sat down.

After half the team reported their findings, Aiza picked up one of the wallets that were lying on the ground and then she stood up. "I had the distinction of going through many of the wallets that were in the container, and I found this one to be remarkably interesting. It belongs to one Seth Bannon, who would be eighty-one years old, if he is still alive somewhere. He was born in Wilkes Barre, Pennsylvania, and the license is dated 1971. His address at that time was in Allentown, Pennsylvania. He was a lawyer who worked for the firm of Trout, Kressley and Levine. I found a second driver's license dated 1927 from the city and state of Wilmington, North Carolina. The wallet also contained bills of various denominations, dated from 1921 to 1970. I found pictures of what are presumably his wife and children. My best guess is that he disappeared in 1971 and wound up in 1927, and then eventually, arrived at this Time Travel Facility in 2013. None of the other wallets contained any items spanning that long a period of time, although some were quite interesting." She sat down.

8

Finally, it was Peter's turn to speak. He said, "Folks I think we should take a bathroom break at this point and you should grab some drinks. I have an awful lot to share with you this evening."

Fifteen minutes later, he stood up. "I have read Nelson Wainwright's journal and I took a lot of notes. First, I will tell you about the Time Travel Facility. Back in 1987, an amateur spelunker, named Lawrence Delp, found a wormhole in a cave. After a bit of trepidation, he decided to step through a shimmering, green membrane and he wound up in 1933, finding the year on a newspaper in the town. He spent a couple of days in the past and then returned to 1987. He informed his former superiors at the CIA and after twenty years of research, they found the way to send TTIs back to the time periods where people had been trapped for lengthy periods of time. In 2001, Nelson Wainwright was offered a position at the facility and in 2007 he was named director."

Peter went on to tell the story of General Rodin and the cast of characters that followed him into the past. He then shared several of the stories of the bouncers, as told to Nelson in 2013 when they all returned to the facility at the same time, except for Clarissa Fortuna, an author who had traveled for seventy-five years, and General Dan Rodin. "There is a copy of Clarissa's book in our possession, and I hope to read it over the next day or two.

"Somehow, General Rodin traveled to the future, which the experts had not thought possible, but he was there in the form of a hologram, only being seen by one person. He found out that the Time Travel Facility had been destroyed on July 15th, 2013 and he fervently wished that he would be able to get back there before the destruction occurred.

"He managed to make it back and after testing the wormhole, traveling to 1607, he came up with a plan to have everyone in the facility time-travel to save their lives. They would live in the past forever, but at least they would live. I must backtrack now. From July 10th to July 12th, each traveler and employee was escorted to a place in the dining room where they could not be heard by outside sources. Everyone was told not to speak of this to anyone else once they left the dining room. Deciding to leave for the past on July 13th, they rounded everyone up, grabbed weapons and tools, and clothing, and loaded everything in a couple of horse drawn wagons, passing through the membrane moments before armed soldiers broke into the facility, finding nobody there.

"They found this place to build their village, but they still had no idea what time period they found themselves in. Several of the soldiers, along with General Rodin and his twin brother, Harry, took off to see if they could find civilization anywhere nearby. When they returned two weeks later, they informed the travelers that they were in the year 1607 and were approximately fifty-five miles from the Jamestown, Virginia settlement.

"Able to use modern tools that they brought with them; they built a village in short order. Wanting to have a democracy, they elected a mayor, a treasurer, a secretary, and a sheriff. When the first traveler died in 1614, they voted to cremate all remains, so nothing could be found in the future."

He shared stories of the living conditions and how the community was affected by weather until the journal entries ended in 1627. At that point there were still sixty-nine survivors.

Exhausted from all the information that was thrown at them, by eleven PM, everyone was tucked into their sleeping bags and the camp drew deathly quiet as the final embers of the fire burned out.

9

When the sun rose the next morning, sixteen black-clad men in face paint, began burning the bodies of the archeological team as other men operating heavy equipment destroyed the dig completely, and then replanted trees and shrubs brought in from other areas of the forest.

Yesterday, after the storage box was opened, electronic signals had been sent to a secret underground base five miles away. The facility had been set up in 2013 after the mass escape from the TTF. Upon their hiring, everyone's badge was implanted with a chip that would send a signal when an employee left the facility under unauthorized conditions, and the team of assassins had been waiting eleven years for this to happen.

Author Bio

Larry Deibert has written fourteen books: Combat Boots dainty feet-Finding Love In Vietnam, The Christmas City Vampire, The Other Side Of The Ridge-Gettysburg, June 27th, 2013 to July 2nd, 1863, Family, Fathoms, From Darkness To Light, The Life Of Riley, Santa's Day Jobs, Werewolves In The Christmas City, The Christmas City Angel, Witches Werewolves And Walter, The Other Side Of The Ridge, New York 1930, A Christmas City Christmas, and this book, The Other Side Of The Ridge, New York City, September 10th and 11th, 2001, all published by Kindle Direct Publishing https://kdp.amazon.com/en_US/

He is a Vietnam veteran and is the past president of the Lehigh Northampton Vietnam Veterans Memorial in Macungie, Pa.

Larry retired from the U.S. Postal Service in 2008 after working as a letter carrier for over 21 years

He and his wife, Peggy, live in Hellertown, Pa., where he enjoys reading and writing. They love traveling and have visited such places as California, Hawaii, North Carolina, Scotland, and England.

Larry's website is www.larryldeibert.com

You may contact Larry at larrydeibert@rcn.com Signed copies may be purchased directly from the author. Postage per book is $3.00

Larry Deibert's Books

Family $14
Over the course of 226 years, Revolutionary War soldier, Julian Ross, an immortal, gives the gift to five humans and a three-legged dog named Riley. One of his Family wants to kill him, hoping that he will then have the power to create more immortals.

Combat Boots dainty feet-Finding Love in Vietnam $13
Based on the author's military service, experiences shared by other vets, and the experiences of several nurses, the novel follows the nearly two-year service of Greg Taylor. Drafted at two-hundred and fifty-five pounds, he sheds seventy-nine pounds over seventeen weeks of training. Six months later he is sent to Vietnam and rekindles a romance with a girl he knew before going in the army. She is an

officer and their affair is illicit in the eyes of the army. They become engaged and return home together, however not as either of them had expected.

Santa's Day Jobs $13
In this children's Christmas book, Santa takes a year off, performing twelve different jobs. With beautiful illustrations by Ashley Reigle, the text is written for kids from 6 to 99. The second part of the book contains the original black and white drawings, suitable for coloring. The text is written by kids.

The Christmas City Vampire $13
In 2010, between Black Friday and Christmas Eve, a vampire must slay five beautiful, young women in order to end a one-hundred and fifty-year curse. On Christmas Day, two other mythical creatures have been discovered in Bethlehem.

Werewolves In The Christmas City $13
Five years after being captured, two werewolves are living as humans in Bethlehem. A third werewolf has been released from three-hundred years of captivity. The trio is captured by a rogue military group hell bent on creating werewolf clones to fight our wars. The experiments go awry, and the imitation creatures terrorize Bethlehem.

The Christmas City Angel $13
In 2018, God sends an angel to Bethlehem to change the lives of several people. Newspaper man, Russ Gallagher, figures out who she is and finds out about the people Victoria Christmas has helped in the past. A half dozen of my FB friends have contributed their true-life angel stories, and I share what happened to my daughter when she was

about five. Christmas is the time for miracles, and you are sure to find a few.

A Christmas City Christmas $12

Julian and Petra Ross and their dog, Riley, three immortals from my novel, *Family*, arrive in Bethlehem to attend the funeral of a friend. A retro toy store is facing closure until the owners purchase a truck load of somewhat magical toys. A Santa porch pirate is arrested, but his heroism in a recent war is discovered. Julian Ross gives the gift of immortality to at least one human, changing her life forever.

From Darkness To Light $11

God assigns eight humans the task of sending all earthbound spirits to their final reward, be it Heaven or Hell. The team utilizes interesting weapons and tools to complete their mission. Before it is all over, four more humans join the fray and at least one of them dies, but everyone's lives are changed forever.

Witches, Werewolves And Walter $10

In 2016, six months after all the werewolves were slain, retired Bethlehem Police detective Hyram Lasky and his wife, Susan are vacationing in Wrightsville Beach, North Carolina. Unbeknownst to them, two werewolf clones have survived and, along with a human lacky, they have relocated to Wilmington, North Caroline where they are expecting a litter of the mythical creatures. Three evil witches, triplets, are trying to destroy their three sisters, who are good witches. Walter, an earthbound spirit is trying to get sent to his final reward. The Lasky's, missing four limbs between them, get together with a team of humans, selected by God to destroy Satan's minions in a final battle of good versus evil.

The Other Side Of The Ridge-Gettysburg, June 27th, 2013 to July 2nd, 1863 $9
Black retired Brigadier General Daniel Rodin is thrust into the past by a weather anomaly. He is captured by Confederates and confronted by Robert E. Lee. After reading Rodin's journal, he accepts the fact that the general is indeed from the future. With the assistance of future time travelers and his twin brother, Harry, he must get back to his time before he changes the course of the war.

The Other Side Of The Ridge-New York, 1930
After surviving Gettysburg, Daniel Rodin is transported through time, winding up on the top floor of the unfinished Empire State Building. Again, along with future time travelers, he helps to stop a team of criminals from stealing nearly two million dollars.

Fathoms $7
In 1944, a sailor disappears from the Battleship North Carolina. Seventy years later, his widow, his grandson, his grandson's wife, several of his long dead shipmates and several other interesting characters solve the mystery.

The Life Of Riley $6
Written in his voice, this is the story about my late dog Riley. In the time I knew him he had many adventures and misadventures he wanted to share with his readers.